Elk Grove Village Public Library

1 Rev. Morrison Boulevard
Elk Grove Village, Illinois

FINES-5¢ PER DAY ADULT BOOKS
3¢ PER DAY JUVENILE BOOKS

WHAT I TELL YOU
THREE TIMES IS FALSE

Books by Samuel Holt

ONE OF US IS WRONG
I KNOW A TRICK WORTH TWO OF THAT
WHAT I TELL YOU THREE TIMES IS FALSE

WHAT I TELL YOU THREE TIMES IS FALSE

SAMUEL HOLT

TOR

WHAT I TELL YOU THREE TIMES IS FALSE

Copyright © 1987 by Samuel Holt

First printing: February 1987

A TOR Book

Published by Tom Doherty Associates, Inc.
49 West 24 Street
New York, N.Y. 10010

ISBN: 0-312-93004-6

Library of Congress Catalog Card Number: 86-50959

Printed in the United States of America

0 9 8 7 6 5 4 3 2 1

This is for Breckenridge, from Edwin

1

Sometimes I think I can fly a plane.

Which is silly, of course, but I'm reminded of it
every time I'm aboard a small aircraft, some six- or
eight-seat puddle jumper. On jumbo jets I mind my own
business, consider myself just as much a parcel as anybody else, and have no fantasies about sitting up front
among all the dials and switches. But when I find
myself in a small plane, I invariably get into this completely inaccurate sense of myself as being a pilot.

It's because I *played* a pilot, of course; Jack Packard
had his own single engine Beechcraft. On PACKARD,
the highly successful television series that made me rich
and then typecast me so thoroughly that I haven't found
work since, I played a fellow of many parts. Jack
Packard, criminologist, college professor, karate black
belt, and amateur detective, had lots of skills and talents
that I shared with him only through the camera's
connivance.

I was reminded of all this once again when Bly and I

deplaned at Toncontin Airport in Tegucigalpa and were ushered across the field toward the two-engine Cessna that would take us on to Munro's Island. That would be our third plane today, but the only one small enough to trigger my fantasy.

We had begun with an early-morning Delta flight from sunny Los Angeles to cloudy and humid New Orleans, where we'd just barely made our connection with a TACA flight to Central America. At its first stop, Belize City in Belize, there was light rain from a very bruised-looking sky, but here in Tegucigalpa, Honduras, there was no precipitation at the moment. Wet tarmac indicated rain in the past and menacing low clouds sprawled on the mountaintops suggested more of it in the near future, but we'd been given a rain-free time out for our changeover to plane number three.

A brown-uniformed airport employee, all smiles and bows for the VIP—me—led us across, and a pair of grumpy baggage handlers in gray jumpsuits followed with a cart containing our luggage. Ahead was the Cessna, white with purple trim. Three people stood beside it, watching us approach.

I recognized Harriet Fitzgerald, naturally, though we'd never met. Over the last ten or fifteen years, she has played Agatha Christie's Miss Marple so often in movies and television—and once onstage, in Los Angeles, at the Dorothy Chandler Pavilion, in a failed play that will remain forever pre-Broadway—that she has by now eclipsed Margaret Rutherford's association with the part and virtually *become* Miss Marple, as I have apparently become Jack Packard. She is also, I believe, like me, considered unemployable in any other role.

We arrived, and the brown-uniformed man, in harshly

accented English, introduced the pilot, one Ralph Mc-
Closkey, an easygoing and somewhat beefy American,
who shook my hand and grinned, saying, "I was a
regular viewer. Very pleased to meet you."

"Thanks. This is my friend, Bly Quinn."

Bly and the pilot exchanged a handshake and a few
words while the brown-uniformed man bowed himself
away and the two grumpy luggage handlers stowed all
the gear through the small door at the right rear of the
fuselage. I turned to Harriet Fitzgerald, stuck out my
hand, and said, "Ah, Miss Marple, at last we meet."

She smiled slightly, and gave me a firm handshake.
"Professor Packard," she said in her midlantic accent,
not quite American, not quite English, "this *is* a pleasure. And this is *my* friend, Daphne Wheeler."

Daphne Wheeler was more obviously lesbian, by which
I mean she had made more of an effort to appear to be a
lesbian, from the close-cropped gray hair and absolute
lack of makeup to the bulky flannel shirt—in this climate!
—and gray-green corduroy trousers and hiking shoes.
Both women were fairly short and heavyset, but Harriet
Fitzgerald was more fussily feminine, suiting the part
she most often played. Off-camera, however, the fuzzy,
frizzy hairdo and bunches of lace and vaguely doughy
features were belied by a cold, clear eye and a hint of
sardonic smile around the mouth and a very firm set of
the shoulders.

As I tipped the luggage men—they remained grumpy—
the pilot said, "Just waiting for one more, then we'll be
off."

"This is an American-registered plane," Bly said.

McCloskey grinned at her. Bly being a very good-looking healthy blonde, men frequently grin at her. "That's right," he said.

She pointed to the registration number on the Cessna's wing. "I could tell because it starts with N," she said. "And I know British planes have numbers that start with V, but I've never known why."

"Victoria," McCloskey told her. "She was queen when the registration system started."

"That's wonderful," Bly said. She makes her living writing scripts for television sitcoms, but stray facts are her real love. "A little historical leftover. But why N for American planes? Before Nixon, was there ever a president with a last name starting with N?"

"No," Harriet Fitzgerald said.

McCloskey said, "Registration started because planes could cross borders so easily, unseen and unregulated. American planes mostly crossed borders southward. The Spanish-language radio operators couldn't pronounce the U in United States."

Bly stared at him, delighted. "No! Is that true? Nited States?"

"Like MOS," I said, trying to enter the conversation.

Bly impatiently shook her head. "I already know that one."

"Of course you do," I told her. "You're a scriptwriter."

"*I* don't," McCloskey said. "What's MOS?"

"In American movie and television scripts," I explained, "if a scene is to be shot silent, for sound effects or whatever to be put in later, the notation at the head of the scene is MOS, and it comes from the very early days of sound movies. A script girl invented it while taking down instructions from Erich Von Stroheim, and it means 'Mit Out Sound.' "

McCloskey laughed and said, "Okay. Same as Nited States." Then he looked at his watch, looked at the sky, looked over at the terminal building, and said, "I wish he'd hurry up. We're supposed to be getting weather pretty soon."

"Who are we waiting for?" I asked.

"Somebody named French."

That would be Jack French, whom I had never met but had heard of. A former director of commercials in New York, he'd become a director of miniseries more recently in Los Angeles, and would direct our promo. He was supposed to be very good and very fast, but also very highly strung.

Bly said, "Where's he coming from?"

"He was on your flight out of New Orleans," McCloskey said. "I don't know what happened to— Wait a minute, is this him?"

It was. The brown-uniformed escort approached again, this time trotting along beside a skinny man with long black hair who ran like a confirmed jogger. They arrived in a dead heat, and the brown-uniformed man gasped out an introduction to McCloskey, who introduced the rest of us. Jack French had deep lines creasing his cheeks and forehead, which made him look worried and semi-starved. He looked older than fifty, but was probably younger than forty, and he had a high-pitched buzzing voice when he said, "I'm sorry, I'm a nervous traveler, my stomach gets all, I had to make a brief stop there."

"What you want," Daphne Wheeler told him, "is a good stiff drink before you travel."

"I don't drink," French told her, looking very solemn. "I'm an alcoholic."

"Oh," Daphne Wheeler said, while the rest of us shifted around in embarrassment.

"Well, let's get aboard," McCloskey said with another look skyward. "Mr. Holt, if you and Miss Quinn would take the rear seats, then Miss Fitzgerald and Miss Wheeler the middle seats, and Mr. French, you'll be up front with me."

"Oh, not me," French said. "Let me sit in back. I don't want to see what's going on."

I would have loved to sit up front, next to the real pilot, but it would have been childish to say so. I simply stood there, smiling, waiting to be called upon, and Bly said, "Switch seats with me, I love to sit in front."

Drat. Bly didn't come off as particularly childish, *and* she got to sit up front. French and I climbed into the plane, crawled over the other seats, and settled down in the rear. The space just behind us was crammed with luggage.

I'm six foot six, so I find most means of transportation rather cramped, and this little plane was far from being an exception. I also didn't like the way Jack French kept gulping and grimacing and swallowing and clutching his elbows from the instant McCloskey started the first engine. This final leg of the journey was supposed to take a little more than an hour, bringing us to Munro's Island sometime before six, and I could hardly wait to get it over with.

Bumpity bumpity bumpity, the Cessna waddled out to the runway, feeling very full and very heavy. We had no windows back here, which I'm sure French liked. McCloskey revved his engines one last time before take-off, I strained futilely to see what was going on past Harriet Fitzgerald's fuzzy-haired head, and Jack French gulped and gulped beside me. "I don't know why I ever agreed to this," he muttered, just barely audible above the engine roar. "I don't even *like* cancer."

2

Here was the idea: In a mysterious mansion on a mysterious island, four famous fictional detectives prowl around, behaving in ways appropriate to their characters. What are they doing? Looking for a cure for cancer. But the American Cancer Society has a better way: Scientific research financed by *your* tax-deductible contributions.

Like Jack French, I, too, was unsure what had made me agree to get involved in this thing. Generally speaking, I say no to appeals to give my time to charitable promotions, preferring to give money, since otherwise my time would very rapidly fill up with nothing but public service work. Rather than have to choose to whom I should say yes or no, I let a blanket refusal protect me. Also, I'm doing my best to *end* my association in the public mind with Jack Packard. It's been more than three years since PACKARD went off the air—it was still as popular as ever, but all of us on the show had simply run out of steam—and I am yet to find any other acting work at all. Not that I need the money, since PACKARD reruns will keep me quite comfortable indeed for the foreseeable future, but because I want the work. Retirement at age thirty-four, regardless of how rich and cushy that retirement might be, is goddamn boring.

But Zack Novak, my agent, had really pushed for me to do this Cancer Society spot. "Danny and Mort *always* have new projects coming along," he'd pointed out. "You do them this favor, you get to know them in their own home, then farther down the line I can give them a call, present you as a strong possibility for this or that or the other."

This, or that, or the other. The conversation had taken place in August, a month ago, and I'd been in my New York townhouse at the time, on West 10th Street in the Village, a vantage point from which everything connected with Hollywood and television looks weird and distorted and—I'm far from the first person to notice this—very much like something in *Alice in Wonderland*. Eat Me. Drink Me. Trust Me. "Zack," I said, "I'm trying to get *away* from Packard."

"You use what you've got to reach what you want," he told me at his most avuncular. Zack clothes himself in Savile Row suits and courtly mannerisms, so when he shows his killer-shark side, it always surprises people.

"Listen," I said, "I have Anita here, we're just about to go out to the island for a couple days."

"Enjoy, dear boy," he told me. "And say hello to the lovely restaurateur."

"I will." Anita, the lovely restaurateur herself, impatiently paced the office behind my back, working off nervous energy.

"And while you're basking in the Southampton sun," Zack went on, "think about Danny and Mort."

"I suppose I will," I admitted.

As I hung up and got to my feet, Anita stopped her pacing, put her hands on her hips, gave me a hard look, and said, "Why is it, when Zack wants you to do something you don't want to do, you never just say *no*?"

"I do say *no*," I protested. "He just never hears it."

My office is on the second floor of the house, with windows overlooking 10th Street between Fifth and Sixth Avenues. I have a double-sided desk in front of those windows, with chairs on both sides, so that I can sit with my back to the view when I'm serious about getting work done, or sit facing the view when I'm just kidding myself. We'd been in the office because I was looking for the name of a new restaurant in Amagansett that had been recommended to me and that I'd written down on a little piece of paper somewhere, and when Zack had phoned I'd sat facing the view because I already knew, as Anita had pointed out, that I wouldn't want to do it, whatever it was, and that Zack wouldn't listen to me say no.

"All right," Anita said, but then her impatience took hold again, and she said, "Come on, let's go. How many new restaurants can there be in Amagansett since last year? We'll just ask."

"Hundreds," I said, but I knew she was impatient because she so rarely took time off from *her* restaurant, and if she was out here in the world for a Monday-through-Wednesday getaway, she wanted to *get away*, dammit, and not hang around in some dark room listening to a client fail to impose his opinion on his agent. A tall and striking woman, slender almost to boniness, Anita Imperato ignores her own sharp good looks and probably keeps her figure mostly because she's around food so much she feels contempt for it. She's run her small Abingdon Square restaurant, Vitto Impero, ever since she threw her ne'er-do-well husband out seven years ago, and apart from her edgily ironic belief that a Greenwich Village Italian girl like her shouldn't be hanging out with a TV celebrity, she's the perfect counterpoint to the New York half of my life.

So we left. The rental car from the place I use on West 56th Street was waiting down by the curb, a black Mercury Marquis. The driver was someone I knew, though not by name; remembering me, he'd already slid the driver's seat back as far as it would go, to accommodate my long legs. He rode in back as we drove uptown, swinging by 56th Street to drop him off at the rental place, and then took the 59th Street Bridge and Queens Boulevard out of the city to Grand Central Parkway. We could have flown out from Flushing, but when the weather's good and the traffic's light I enjoy the drive.

The late morning sun smiled on delivery vans and limos alike, the air was August warm and soft, the planes lifted off like air balloons from LaGuardia Airport on our left toward destinations that could be no more pleasant than our own, and Anita waited until we were past the city and rolling out across Nassau County before she said, "What *was* that call about? Not Packard in dinner theater again."

"No, no," I assured her. "That idea's dead. Of embarrassment, I think."

"All I could hear was your half of the conversation,"

she pointed out, "and you were mostly saying, 'Yes,
Massa.'"

"Aw, come on."

"You're right." She nodded, conceding the point.
"There was the occasional, 'Gee, Massa,' as well. What
did Zack want you to do?"

"American Cancer Society." I repeated the plot run-
down Zack had given me.

She nodded, watching traffic. Anita drives whether
she's behind the wheel or not. When I was finished with
my description, she said, "So why not do it?"

That astonished me. "You know why," I told her.
"I'm stuck to Packard like Brer Fox to the tar baby."

"But this isn't about Packard," she said. "Or about
Sam Holt, either. This is about cancer."

"It puts Packard and Sam Holt together again on your
television screen," I insisted. "Just what the world
needs now."

"Jesus, listen to you," she said. "This isn't a play,
or a series, or anything like that. They're asking you to
do twenty seconds of airtime in a good cause, that's all,
with a lighthearted reprise of the character you used to
do. It doesn't hurt your goddamn *career* to be some help
to somebody."

When I gave her a quick peek from the corners of my
eyes, her gaze at me was very stern indeed. I said,
"Stop thinking about myself for a minute, huh?"

"Something like that."

"Ask myself, how many people are there in the world
that could be of this kind of use."

"Now you're getting there," she told me, and when I
glanced over again, she was grinning, the grin that

forgives my being a little slow sometimes because I am, after all, cute.

"It should be an interesting place to visit, anyway," I said.

"There's that," she agreed.

"Come along with me," I suggested, though I knew she wouldn't.

"No time," she said, as I'd known she would. "That restaurant doesn't run itself, you know. Take the tennis player."

Mmm. Anita and Bly have never met, which we all think of as a good idea, but they are aware of each other. It's complicated enough to be involved with two women on two coasts three thousand miles apart in the first place; I'm not going to make matters worse by lying to anybody. This arrangement grew of itself, without anybody planning it, and though it usually works out reasonably well, the living isn't always easy. I suppose there's some of the same selfishness at work that Anita had just jabbed me for in connection with the Cancer Society spot, but the fact is, I could not possibly choose either Anita or Bly to give up, and neither one of them wants to give up on me—at least, not so far—so we just go along and try not to worry about it. And on those rare occasions when one of them makes a glancing reference to the other—rather like a glancing blow in the Golden Gloves—I just watch the scenery go by and listen to the silence for a while. As I did this time, and the next thing Anita said had to do with the people we were visiting, so that was that.

And yes, of course, Bly was the sensible one to bring along. It's true she plays tennis, but that isn't the main point about her—that was just Anita getting in a little dig about the contrast between my hearty California girl and my sharp New York girl—the main point about Bly being that as a freelance writer for TV sitcoms, she would have the looseness of schedule that would permit her to get away for an oddball experience like this.

And so, what with one thing and another, here we were crammed into this airplane, and here I was off to play at Jack Packard yet again.

In addition to Packard and Miss Marple, the script for this thing also called for the presence of Sherlock Holmes and Charlie Chan, in the persons of the actors most recently associated with those sleuths. Clement Hasbrouck makes a wonderful Sherlock Holmes, with that chiseled Basil Rathbone look, but he isn't quite as brisk as Rathbone, giving Holmes a statelier, slower manner that seems dull at first but is probably closer to the spirit of the Conan Doyle stories. And Fred Li is not only an improvement on previous Chans by being an actual Oriental, but he has a serenity of manner that makes all those fake aphorisms—"No tree in the forest bears cooked rice" is in one of the original books, for instance—actually seem to make sense.

Jack Packard is the most recently invented of these fictions, and the only one to have originated on television, so I suppose I should have felt pleased and flattered on Jack's account, but my primary reaction as we flew northeastward out over the Caribbean and beneath the gathering stormclouds was a suspicion that James Garner and Tom Selleck had both said no.

3

Afterward, Bly told me how exciting the flight had been, with the heavy clouds pressing lower and lower, the little two-engine Cessna buzzing along just above the choppy waves, that vast low-ceilinged room of air stretched out everywhere between cloud and sea, occasional squalls stippling fat raindrops across the windshield, no trace of land visible for nearly an hour, until McCloskey had leaned close to her, pointing forward, shouting over the engine noise, "There's your island!"

I wish I could have seen it. Stuck back there with the gray-faced Jack French, no windows, crammed up with my knees in my chest and nowhere to put my arms, I only knew for sure that I was in hell. Which particular neighborhood of hell I didn't know, and didn't care.

But Bly, up front, had a grandstand seat. McCloskey was getting weather reports constantly on his radio, every one of them worse and more disagreeable. This was, after all, September, the height of hurricane season, and we were pegging steadily toward that empty part of the ocean where hurricanes are born. This was McCloskey's second trip to the island today—this morning, he'd ferried a group who'd reached Tegucigalpa via the Miami plane—and he assured Bly he would be glad when this day was over. He didn't know the half of it, poor bastard.

But then at last Munro's Island came into view; or at least it came into view for those who had windows. Bly described to me that first sighting, her squinting through the rain-streaked windshield, trying to follow McCloskey's pointing finger, seeing nothing at first but the whitecaps against the gray-black sea, the light colorless and uncertain. Then, all at once, there it was, one black crag sticking up out of the stormy ocean, looking cold and unhuman until, as they—as *we,* I guess—flew nearer, she could make out the amber-lit windows in the house on the cliff. "Boy, did they look good!" she told me later. I bet they did.

We landed in a whipping rain, and in back I could feel the Cessna being jerked around as we descended toward the narrow concrete landing strip on the island's only patch of flat low ground. Jack French had passed from gray to green and was now staring fixedly at the back of Daphne Wheeler's head, teeth clenched. When we hit hard and bounced, and bounced again, a moan leaked out through those teeth, and when he lifted his head, I could see his Adam's apple jumping like a puppy in a sack. But at last we rolled to a stop, and French sighed, and closed his eyes. I thought he was heroic, and I was grateful to him.

McCloskey stayed in his seat, eager to get going—a tropical storm had unexpectedly gathered itself together in the last hour or so and was starting to move westward, toward us—while the rest of us climbed out, to be met by two men in yellow slickers and hats, who had with them several more slickers and hats. We put them on, and I looked around as best I could in the wind and rain. Very close on the right, just past the edge of the concrete runway, sand angled down to a beach, and there was the ocean. Almost as close on the left was the steep cliffside, covered with black-green shrubbery shaking itself in the storm.

One of the men who'd met us called in to the pilot, "You want to stay? The radio says it's getting rough!"

But McCloskey shook his head. "I'll keep in front of it!" he shouted.

"Whatever you say," the man told him, shut his door, and turned to us. "George will bring up the luggage," he said, shouting over the wind. "Come on along and get dry."

So we followed him, as behind us the second man— George, apparently—busily transferred all the luggage from the plane to a rough wooden cart. The first man led us to the cliff, and then around a bit to the right, and there was an elevator. Or not exactly an elevator, but a kind of cable car on tracks, a large square room with railroad-type wheels on the outside of its slanted rear wall. When we were all aboard, with the windowed doors shut, the man pushed a lever and we were winched slowly and smoothly up the steeply angled side of the cliff.

"There it goes," Bly said.

The car we were in had windows on three sides, which was probably a better idea in good weather. As we rose, more and more of the island and the surrounding ocean became visible and there, as Bly had said, was the little white and purple Cessna, climbing up sharply through the air, struggling for altitude. All at once it side-slipped, the right wing knifing down toward the water, and everybody in our car went very tense, but McCloskey was a good pilot. He fought his plane level again, skipped through the spume above the whitecaps, and at last managed to curve up and out and away, running off westward toward the Central American coast.

"He should have stayed," the man said, and pulled off his yellow cap. Short and neat, he had a small and almost delicate-looking skull with thin light blond hair. His eyebrows were so pale as to be invisible over washed-out blue eyes. His nose was narrow and long, his lips narrow and wide, his skin pale and bloodless. Smiling at us, he said, "Not the best day for a visit, I'm afraid. I'm Danny Douglas."

One of the owners of this place, in other words. Danny Douglas and his partner, Mort Weinstein, were television producers whose company, Danmor Forever, did sitcoms and movies of the week and very occasionally a low budget theatrical movie. They or their company had bought Munro's Island about a year ago at a government auction, the island having been impounded when its previous owner, a thug out of Detroit called Sonny Trager, went to jail on a number of drug charges. He'd had a cocaine-refining plant here, and had used the island as a way station for smuggling from Colombia up into the States. Actual sovereignty over the island apparently resided with Great Britain, which found no reason to interfere. I suspected, but couldn't say for sure, that Danmor Forever was getting some sort of governmental assistance or approval or something in return for making the place available for the Cancer Society promo.

Introductions were made on the way up the side of the cliff, and then repeated all over again at the top, when we met Danny Douglas's partner. The end of the ride took the car up through the bottom of the house to finish at one end of a wide observation room cantilevered out over the cliff, with an incredible view of the sea, and with most of the bulk of the house up behind us. At Danny's instructions, we'd removed our slickers and hats on the way up and hung them with some others on hooks on the car's rear wall, so now we followed him out of the car and turned left. The long room was in front of us, with the view through double-paned glass on our right. Several people were standing in the room, drinks in their hands.

Danny introduced Mort Weinstein, a short hairy bear of a man, stocky, with thick curly black hair that spilled all over his head and flowed down into a bristling beard and moustache. Thick black-rimmed glasses completed the impression of someone hiding behind an impenetrable disguise. But he was actually cheerful and outgoing, pumping everybody's hand, grinning down there inside all that hair, talking in a soft burry baritone, telling us how swell we were to come here.

It was Mort who finished the round of introductions. The other four people present were Clement Hasbrouck (Sherlock Holmes), with his tiny nervous-looking wife, Betsy, and Fred Li (Charlie Chan), with a beautiful black girl I knew I'd seen somewhere before. Her name was Crosby Tucker, and then I remembered: She was a singer, a torch song belter on the Las Vegas show circuit.

"We're it, for the moment," Mort finished, gesturing around at the eleven of us. "Plus George. The tech people and equipment are supposed to fly in tomorrow, but if this storm doesn't blow over, I don't know.''

We all looked out the large plate-glass windows at the storm, which didn't at all look as though it would blow over. As we did so, the cable car doors opened again and George appeared, dragging the cartful of luggage. Without his slicker and cap, George turned out to be a tall muscular black man in his thirties. He said something to Danny about putting the luggage in the guest rooms, and I heard the soft lilting accent of the British Caribbean.

Meantime, Mort invited us to have drinks, and Jack French announced again that he was an alcoholic. "Jack Daniel's and soda," I said, with maybe a bit too much emphasis.

Mort went off with our drink orders, and I looked around at this room, which was about thirty feet wide and ten feet deep, furnished with Oriental carpets on the dark wood floor and lots of wicker, with a gray stone wall at the back. Side tables contained magazines, decks of cards, and boxed games, and one table was itself a backgammon board. A small bar stood near a table containing shortwave radio equipment. Beachlike abstracts in pastels were hung at intervals along the back wall. The overall effect was welcoming and homey, almost front-porchlike, in surprising contrast to all that open air and empty sea just outside.

Clement Hasbrouck stood beside me, looking out at the storm. His profile was very noble. "How strange all this is indeed," he said, in his sonorous radio-announcer voice. Like Harriet Fitzgerald, his accent was almost American and almost English without being exactly either. "Who would ever have imagined to wash up in such an unbelievable place?"

"I was just thinking the same thing," I told him.

He smiled up at me, a tinge of sadness in his smile. (He was reasonably tall, about six feet, but most people smile up at me.) "You and I, of course," he said, "labor under a kind of benign curse, do we not?"

"We do?"

"As other sinners have their crosses to bear, we have our characters."

"Oh, I see," I said. Something deep inside me winced.

"If it were not for Sherlock Holmes," he went on, "I would certainly not be here, would never actually witness this overawing sight."

"I guess that's true."

"How Sherlock drives me," he said, again with that sad smile. "He has taken over my life, for better or worse. A hard taskmaster, and yet see"—with a graceful gesture at the view—"the rewards he gives me. And yet again, still a hard taskmaster."

On Hasbrouck's other side, his tiny wife, Betsy, gave a nervous giggle and said, "Oh, Clement, you love being Sherlock, you know you do."

"But of course," he said, looking down his nose at her. (She flinched, smiling gamely.) "I have just said so. Sherlock has made our very lives possible, my dear, and I hope I'm grateful. Still, the yoke of another man's invention does at times rest heavy on one's shoulders. I'm sure Mr. Holt understands what I'm saying."

"Sure," I said, but wanting to get away from this conversation. A little off, Bly was talking with Fred Li and Crosby Tucker, and seemed to be having more fun. I had remembered hearing Clement Hasbrouck referred to more than once as Clement Hasbeen. Was this my own future I was listening to? Would I eventually give up the struggle to be a working actor, would I just settle comfortably into Jack Packard the rest of my life? In a subtle but clear manner, Hasbrouck was dressed as Sherlock Holmes might under these circumstances; would I wind up doing that, wearing Jack Packard's tweed jackets with the leather elbow patches? I was very glad to see Mort Weinstein approach with my drink.

"One nice thing," he said, as I took my Jack Daniel's and soda, "we're totally self-contained here. Storms come and storms go, but this house goes on forever."

"How rashly you challenge fate," Clement Hasbrouck told him.

"We have our own generator," Mort said, unfazed, "our own deep fresh-water well, and supplies to last us six months. The house is stone, quarried out of the mountain, giving us lots of sub-basements for storage plus the strongest construction you can imagine. If I can tempt fate now, it's because the builders didn't tempt fate when they put the place together."

I asked, "Who built it?"

"Sonny Trager, the drug king." Down inside the heavy beard and moustache, Mort attempted a sly grin, which just barely made it to the surface. "Cocaine money buys the best," he said.

"Sherlock found cocaine quite valuable," Hasbrouck said, nodding seriously.

"Hello? Hello?"

We all turned, to see Danny Douglas over at the radio, microphone in one hand as he held a small receiver tight to his ear. "What now?" Mort said, and headed over toward his partner. The rest of us followed.

Danny was saying, *"Ralph? Ralph? I can hardly hear you!"*

I turned to look out the windows. Great dirty Conestoga wagons of cloud roiled and rolled like speeded-up film over the sea, lower than ever. Not a bird was visible out there, not a light, nothing on the surface of the water, nothing alive beyond the dripping windows.

Mort asked what was going on, and Danny said, "The storm came in too fast, Ralph can't make it back to the coast. He's going to try to land here."

"Here?" Mort's surprise and disbelief said it all.

Danny shouted into the microphone, *"Can you see our lights? Ralph?"*

"The strip has lights," Mort said, and trotted down to the end of the room by the cable car to turn on three or four switches.

I stood by the window, Bly beside me. As it grew darker out there, I could see the room behind me reflected in the glass, and then beyond that reflection the shades of gray of the outer world. Harriet Fitzgerald and Daphne Wheeler were down to my left, with Fred Li and Crosby Tucker beyond, all looking out at the storm. To my right were Clement and Betsy Hasbrouck, and beyond them Mort Weinstein. Reflected in the glass were Danny Douglas, crouched over the radio, and Jack French, hunched on the edge of a wicker chair, sideways to the view. His left hand was balled in his lap, his right hand forward, fingertips drilling on a small glass-topped wicker coffee table. His face was in shadow, and he intently, determinedly, watched his fingers tapping.

"There he is!" Crosby Tucker said, her voice loud and excited. "Oh, that poor son of a bitch!"

Yes. There he was, coming from off to the right, the

little white plane looking as small as a sea gull out there, as defenseless as a Kleenex thrown out a car window. He came hurtling through the middle of the air, not much higher than we were, jolting up and down and slipping from side to side as the winds took him.

We couldn't see the landing strip from here. Our view faced south, and the strip would be around to the right, on the west side of the island. We watched McCloskey try to make the turn, but then the wind grabbed his wings and flung him wide, and for just a second it looked as though he'd come crashing directly through these windows. But then he managed to lift himself up and away, and we looked at his undercarriage before he disappeared over the top of the house without a sound.

That was the strange thing. The double-paned glass and the solid construction of the place meant we hadn't been hearing the storm as it had grown, but I never became aware of that until the Cessna went by, probably no more than forty feet above the window, and we didn't hear a thing. A roaring plane, a roaring storm, and for us it was a silent movie.

Danny still shouted into the radio, though there was nothing he or any of us could do. Jack French hadn't changed position. The Cessna appeared again, off to our left, making a great spiral downward over the ocean toward the landing strip to our right.

He never made it. He was directly in front of us, out over the sea, and just a bit lower than our level, when the wind apparently gusted up at him, lifting his nose. He fought it down again, but then the wind abruptly left him alone, and down he shot toward the whitecaps. He made a sharp left turn, heeling over, trying to grab back some altitude, but the left wingtip touched the water—

from here, it looked as though that's all it did, just tapped the water lightly—and that was the end. The wing ripped off the fuselage, taking one engine with it. The plane flew on for two or three seconds, then angled down. Never slackening speed, it rammed into the water at a steep angle, the fuselage diving straight down through the waves, the second wing stripping off on the way, lying flat on the roiled surface for a second or two more, and then disappearing.

Gone. Not a thing left, not a sign. I could hear Jack French's fingernails on the coffee table glass.

4

We were a subdued group shown to our rooms in the guest wing, contained in its own separate tower, on the east side of the building. Mort showed us up a broad stone staircase with framed movie posters incongruously on the pale walls (Danmor Forever productions, of course), and at its top was a long parlor with tall windows at both ends showing the stormy sky. Comfortable chairs were grouped around a stone fireplace which was too clean to suggest much use. Gesturing to this fireplace, Mort Weinstein said, "For show only. This island doesn't have a lot of wood. Sonny Trager got carried away sometimes."

With his Charlie Chan intonations, Fred Li said, "If you have a castle, you have to have fireplaces."

Crosby Tucker, her grin ironic, said, "Is that more of your goddamn Oriental wisdom?"

"Absolutely."

Bly said, "I can hardly wait to see the dungeon."

"Oh, there is one," Mort told her. "We'll do a house

tour later, but for now, let me get you all to your rooms.''

There were four of these off the parlor, two on each side. Mort showed the Hasbroucks into the near one on the left, with Jack French next to them. Harriet Fitzgerald was given the room opposite the Hasbroucks, with Daphne Wheeler next door. (I liked the tact in that.) "The rest of you," Mort said, "get to climb some more."

Because we were the youngest and healthiest? A smaller staircase continued up, doubling back on itself and opening to a small vestibule, where a delicate little table and an ornate wall mirror were placed between two doors, open to show another pair of guest rooms. Mort distributed us into these, Fred Li and Crosby Tucker on the right, Bly and me on the left. "We'll eat at eight," he told us, "but come on down anytime."

As we closed ourselves into our room, Bly made a face and said, "I dreamed I saw Mandalay."

"Not a happy introduction," I agreed.

She shook her head. "Sam, I don't like anything about this place, not the history, the people here, anything. It isn't just that poor pilot . . . well, it's him, too, of course."

"I know."

"We talked, coming out," she said, and went over to the nearest window to gaze at the storm, as though looking at the place where McCloskey had died would make him more real. "He was a nice guy," she said, her back to me. "He had a good sense of humor. And he didn't come on to me or anything like that."

Something in her voice made me go over and turn her around, to see she was having trouble keeping back the tears. "*Somebody* ought to cry for him," I said, so she did, holding tight to me. Outside the soundproof double-glazed windows, the silent storm rushed around the tower like banshees trying to get in. Inside, a dozen people were scattered through the rooms without a sound to be heard. Then a distant toilet flushed, and in my arms Bly went from tears to laughter. "I heard that," she murmured against my chest.

"Even vampires have to go to the bathroom," I told her.

Rearing back, but still holding to my arms, she showed me her tear-streaked face in its halo of rumpled blond hair. She said, "Thank you, but I do not drink . . . wine."

"All the more for me."

"Dammit, human beings *are* suggestible," she said, and moved away from me, looking around the room. "Where's the john?"

Each guest room had its own full bath, a modern rectangular motel-type room that even included a whirring exhaust fan activated when the light was switched on. While Bly repaired herself in there, I unpacked the luggage George had left on the king-size bed, stowing things away into the walk-in closet and the pair of mirrored dressers. The furniture in this large, comfortable room was modern and simple, with wall-to-wall gray carpeting and matching gray curtains. Sonny Trager had apparently spent some of his cocaine millions on a good interior decorator who didn't feel an overwhelming need to make a statement.

I had never heard of Sonny Trager before this Cancer Society spot had come along, but now that I'd seen the house he'd built himself I wished I knew more about him. It was such a combination of the melodramatic and the prosaic, this craggy turreted stone castle set not on some Carpathian mountaintop but on a rock in the middle of the sea. Probably in good weather much of the melodrama was melted away by Caribbean sun and warmth, but the place would never be mistaken for an ordinary vacation beach house.

Bly had been in that bathroom a long time. I stowed the empty luggage on the top shelf in the closet, came out, and there she was in the bathroom doorway. She was naked. Behind her, running water sounded. Grinning at me, she said, "The shower's big enough for two. Just thought I'd mention it."

And so we established territory.

5

$\mathbb{S}$onny Trager's mad castle consisted of three towers rising from a square fortresslike main structure, which was itself built on a great stone mountain of an island jutting up out of the Caribbean Sea. Trager—or Trager's architects and builders and engineers—had begun by blasting away the craggy peak of the island, slicing away down to a broad square tabletop on which the house would be constructed. The stone they'd cut away was then shaped into blocks and used for the outer walls of the house, supported and strengthened by steel beams shipped out from Mexico. More stone for the exterior was quarried from inside the mountain, creating storerooms and staircases and passageways burrowing deep below the main floor, which was itself fifty feet above the ocean. Some of that space had housed Trager's cocaine-refining plant, now dismantled. Sophisticated generating equipment installed inside the mountain used the constant movement of the sea to create and store electricity. A well more than a hundred feet deep brought up fresh water.

The house itself was a strange combination of modern and traditional, practical and whimsical, and couldn't have been conceived of by anyone with less than unlimited cash. Danny Douglas and Mort Weinstein hadn't owned the place long and hadn't yet done much to replace Trager's vision with their own, so except for their film posters and the pieces they'd brought to furnish their individual offices and bedrooms, the style and sense of the place still evoked the brain of its builder; and an odd brain it seemed to be.

Working fireplaces were in most rooms, though there was no supply of wood. A large room lined with reproductions of medieval banners was actually the game room, equipped with a Ping-Pong table, dart board, pinball machines, and video games. A vast library that could have housed a couple of thousand books contained less than a hundred, half of them paperbacks. The kitchen was huge and modern and wouldn't have been out of place in a large hotel; its capacity was far beyond any need of this house.

As for the towers, all three were conical, reaching up out of the main mass of the house like stalagmites. Ours, on the east, had the four guest rooms and guest parlor on its lowest floor, then the vestibule and two more guest rooms—including the one for Bly and me— one flight up, and another single large dramatic room yet above that, with walls of windows on three sides, giving the impression of being in a balloon in the middle of the sky; not a happy idea in this kind of weather.

The opposite tower, on the west, contained more and smaller rooms and only one full bath per floor, and was meant to be the servants' quarters. George lived there now, and the technical crew for our television spot would be housed there once they arrived.

And finally there was the central tower, on the south, rising up from just behind the observation room. Thicker at its base than the other two, it was taller and more showily craggy, with balconies and deepset windows to give it a dramatic and irregular profile. Our hosts' rooms and offices were up there.

Below the towers were the main rooms, all surrounding a great dining hall, two stories high, with steel beams visible high above, beneath a cathedral ceiling, and windows only in the upper parts of the walls. The idea that Sonny Trager had a baronial view of himself was strongest in this room, with its arched entrances below and arched windows above, rough stone walls and smooth stone floor and massive wooden dining table and chairs, plus that strange cold modern touch of the steel beams where earlier barons would have used wood.

It was in this room where, at eight that evening, the storm still pounding outside, we all gathered for dinner, and where Harriet Fitzgerald and Daphne Wheeler had their bitter quarrel, probably brought on by the strangeness of the place we'd all found ourselves in, and the fresh memory of the sudden awful death of our pilot.

Until their fight, dinner had been an awkwardly quiet affair. No one wanted to be the life of the party so soon after McCloskey's death, so conversation limped and faltered, not helped by the fact we were mostly meeting for the first time, and Danny and Mort, in traditional dinner-party style, had separated couples. I had Crosby Tucker on my left and Betsy Hasbrouck on my right, with Mort beyond Crosby at one end of the table, while

Bly was diagonally opposite me, between Jack French (still looking nervous and bad-tempered and self-absorbed) and George, who was eating with us because it would be ridiculous, with only twelve people on the entire island, to have one of them eat separately from the rest.

Not that George was actually *with* us very much. He and Danny were making and serving dinner together, so both of them were constantly up and down, carrying things to and from the kitchen. That left Bly pretty much on her own, with George's empty chair on her left and Danny's empty chair beyond that at the end of the table, and the silent grouchy Jack French on her other side. Whenever our eyes met, she looked more and more rebellious.

My situation was much better. Leaving mousy little Betsy Hasbrouck to Fred Li, on her other side, I did my talking with Crosby Tucker and Mort Weinstein. Mort, normally a cheerful and witty man down inside all that hair, was rather glum, McCloskey having after all been to some degree a friend of his, but Crosby Tucker was irrepressible, a frank girl whose strong good looks and show biz success had only confirmed her natural self-confidence. She was from Boston originally, her father one of the few black doctors there with a multi-racial practice, and it was clear that self-doubt rarely made much headway with her. She was explaining to Mort, in his role as television producer, why she had turned down the three television series offers she'd so far received—"In front of that camera, you wear out your welcome, but I can do club dates till I'm old enough to hike out onstage with a walker"—and I was reflecting on how my own career proved her right, when Daphne Wheeler suddenly brought all conversation to a halt by saying loudly, "Of course, the great Harriet *Fitzgerald* can do what she *wants*. But don't count on *her* if you really *need* anything."

Bly and I talked it over later, and we both agreed the seating arrangement was the main cause of the trouble. Not that there wasn't disruption between Harriet and Daphne anyway, but our placement at dinner gave Daphne too much solitude in which to brood. It's true that Bly was also left out of things, but Bly at least had started the meal a healthy person in a good frame of mind. The same couldn't be said of Daphne; for instance, while everyone else had changed into clothing appropriate for dinner, she was still dressed like a lumberjack.

But the seating was the main problem, and the rest of it was like this: Between Jack French and Mort Weinstein were Harriet Fitzgerald and Clement Hasbrouck, who had been deep in a solemn comparison of their lives as Miss Marple and Sherlock Holmes ever since we sat down. Then, after Mort and Crosby Tucker and me, there was Betsy Hasbrouck, in conversation with Fred Li, and then Daphne. On that side of her, therefore, was Fred Li's back, and on the other the chair too seldom occupied by Danny Douglas. So Daphne had nothing to do but think about her problems, and eventually choose to attack.

Even so, it might all have been no more than a brief embarrassment, if Harriet hadn't decided the best response was a firm and forceful counterattack. "Daphne," she said, her voice like the crack of doom, "you're tiresome. You're frequently tiresome. I would go so far as to say—"

"I know how far *you'd* go," Daphne cried. "You'd do *anything* to hog the limelight for yourself! If people knew, if people *knew,* if they just knew what I know about the great—"

"Daphne, you will *not* make a spectacle of yourself. I absolutely forbid—"

Oh, yes, she would. Daphne was in full cry now, and nobody was going to absolutely forbid her anything. Remembering her advice to Jack French at the beginning of our final plane ride, always to start a voyage with a good stiff drink, and seeing how blotchily red the woman's face had now become, how her fingers nervously clutched at the cloth as she glared across the table, I began to suspect that the California white wine we were having with our chicken breasts and asparagus tips (from the freezer) was not the only alcohol Daphne had taken on board since our arrival here. So liquor was fueling her, and isolation was fueling her, and long-standing grievances and a suspicion of inferiority were fueling her, and if Harriet Fitzgerald thought there was a hope in hell of Daphne Wheeler not making a spectacle of herself, Harriet was dead wrong.

"Forbid *me!*" cried Daphne, struggling to her feet, knocking over her half-full wineglass. "And just who died and left *you* lord and master? Some nasty fake dyke, that's all, without a particle—"

"Daphne!"

"You don't care for anyone but yourself!" On her feet, weaving, suddenly much more obviously drunk, Daphne pointed a blunt finger at Harriet, crying, "Homosexuality is self-love, don't you realize that? Just—just—just loving one's *self,* one's own sort and self—"

"Daphne, you are raving," Harriet told her, sharp and icy, her eyes cold with fury. "You have already gone too far. Now, stop."

To some extent, Daphne herself seemed to agree that she'd gone too far. She paused slightly, as though going over in her mind what she'd already said. But then she clearly came to the conclusion that having already gone too far, it hardly mattered what else she came out with, so she gave Harriet a theatrically superior smile (somewhat blurred) and said, "That, of course, is why I so often find you repellent. Repellent. Repellent."

Rising, flinging her napkin onto the table, Harriet said, "I will not stay here and—"

"Oh, don't *you* move," Daphne said, waving her hands. "I'm going, I'm going, I'm going." And she backed away from the table, knocking her chair over this time.

Except that the scene was really very painful and embarrassing for everybody in the room, and except for her utter seriousness, Daphne was doing a classic comic drunk act, knocking things over, gesturing too broadly, speaking the unspeakable. Would she go on to the next step in the sequence—trip over her own feet and sprawl on the floor?

No. Up till then, the whole thing had happened so fast and been so startling that nobody else had made a move, but now all at once Danny Douglas, who just before the explosion had returned from the kitchen again with another bottle of wine and sat down, and who was therefore closest (with Fred Li) to Daphne, leaped to his feet, made a lunge for her, grabbed her near elbow, and tugged her back to a shaky equilibrium, saying, "Miss Wheeler, be careful, this floor can be very slippery. I'm sorry, I don't think you feel well."

As soon as Danny made his move, so did Fred and I, though I have no idea what good we thought we'd do,

jumping up and waving our arms at Daphne, who suddenly looked merely confused, as though awakened from
sleepwalking. "I," she said, blinking at Danny, whose
small neat round head was bent toward her in honest
concern. "I, yes, I must be . . ."

Little Betsy Hasbrouck, whom I'd thought of as nothing but mousy and ineffectual, hovering permanently
over the fragile ego of her husband, now showed another side to herself, taking charge, rising up between
Fred and me, moving toward Daphne as she tottered
beside Danny. "It's the long trip," Betsy announced.
"Travel is exhausting for everyone, that's what *I* think.
Daphne, just come with me. There's been far too much
happening today."

"Yes," Daphne said, turning almost blindly toward
this new authoritative voice.

Worried, Danny said, "Will you be all right? Should
I come along?"

"No, we'll be just fine," Betsy said, taking Daphne
by the arm, turning her away from the table, deftly
moving off with her toward the door. Docilely, Daphne
shuffled away, not looking back. Watching them go, I
realized this wasn't a different facet of Betsy Hasbrouck
after all; she was a kind of companion/nurse for her
husband anyway, and was simply using the same skills
now for this new patient.

Betsy and Daphne left. The rest of us sat down again,
in a silence worse and more awkward than ever, and
Danny said, "It *was* a long trip for you all, of course,
very tiring, and then seeing Ralph . . ."

"Daphne is a very stupid person," Harriet interrupted, her manner still coldly furious. "She has been
pestering me and pestering me because I haven't been

able to arrange to get her unpublishable novel published. Well, who could? So, at last, I have had to tell her that after this trip she'll need to find other living arrangements for herself.''

''Dear lady,'' Clement Hasbrouck said, bowing his noble head toward her, ''I know this has been a strain.''

''Not for me,'' Harriet said icily. ''I'm just fine.''

6

Forehead touching the glass of an observation room window, hands cupped around her face to eliminate reflections of the room as she stared outward into the night, Crosby Tucker said, "I can't see a fucking thing out there."

"I don't think anything *is* fucking out there," Fred Li told her. "Not in this storm."

Crosby gave up trying to see the outside world. Turning back to the rest of us, she said, "How long's it supposed to go on, anyway?"

Bly said, "George told me—"

Surprised, I interrupted her, saying, "George? You actually got to talk to him?"

"A word here, a word there," she told me. "Come and go, talking of Michelangelo. Anyway, he said Danny radioed Puerto Rico to report McCloskey's death, and they said Donald's still building, and—"

Clement Hasbrouck, over by the bar, paused in pouring himself a healthy splash of brandy, to frown at Bly and say, "Donald? Who on earth is that?"

"The storm," Bly told him. "It's the fourth of the season, so it's named Donald."

Fred Li said, "It was better when the hurricanes were all named after women. Hurricane Lola. Hurricane Belle. You could really *believe* in a hurricane like that. You get these hurricanes named Jimmy and Bob, who can take them seriously? Everybody knows it's women that are the true natural destructive force in the world."

"Chinese sexists are the worst," Crosby Tucker commented comfortably.

Clement, frowning at the windows, still holding the brandy bottle in one hand and the glass in the other, said, "It's a hurricane, is it?"

"Tropical storm," Bly told him. "But with ambitions."

We five—Fred and Crosby and Clement and Bly and me—had come out to the observation room for after-dinner drinks and conversation, leaving Danny and George happily cleaning up together in the kitchen. Mort Weinstein and Jack French had gone off to Mort's office to discuss details of the shoot we'd be getting to once tropical storm Donald went away and the technical people could fly out with their equipment. As for the others, Betsy Hasbrouck and Daphne Wheeler were presumably still together up in the guest tower, and immediately after dinner Harriet Fitzgerald had marched away alone to her room; no one had asked her to join us instead.

Once we all had drinks, and had tried and failed to see anything past our own reflections in the windows, and had discussed the storm still gathering itself around us, we moved on to the inevitable real topic of conversation. I'd been wondering which of us would bring it up first, expecting either Crosby or Bly to be the one, and was surprised when it was Clement Hasbrouck who started it. Settling himself in a comfortable chair with his drink, looking judicious but tolerant, he said, "I must say, I do feel it would be better for Harriet if she were a bit *more* like Miss Marple in her off hours."

"Oh, I don't know," Fred Li said. His round face was smiling and mischievous, a bit more sardonic and cynical than he permitted himself when being Charlie Chan. Grinning at us all, he said, "I like a good cat fight myself. I was sort of hoping one of them would throw something."

"You were right next to Daphne, smart guy," Crosby pointed out. "If Harriet threw something, you'd get it too."

"Probably most of it," Fred told her, unfazed. "Harriet doesn't look to me like somebody with good aim."

"Nor with particularly good sense, I'm afraid," Clement said. "I had been aware before, of course, in the most indirect way, that there was this certain—irregularity—in Harriet's private life."

"You mean," Fred said, "that she's a diesel dyke."

Bly told him, "I don't think that's exactly right. I think the more butch one is the diesel dyke, and that would be Daphne."

"She's more obvious, certainly," Clement said, "but I wouldn't say she was the stronger or the harder of the two."

Fred Li said, "Not the one with balls, you mean."

"They're a great couple, anyway," Crosby Tucker said. "Did I follow what was going on? Daphne wrote a novel, thought Harriet would use her influence to get it published, and Harriet said no."

"Or," I suggested, "didn't have that kind of influence."

"Anyway," Crosby said, "Daphne nags Harriet, Harriet says she's had enough, Harriet throws Daphne out."

Bly said, "You mean, Harriet threatens to throw Daphne out. I think it was just a power thing to keep Daphne in her place. This was the rebellion tonight, the final gesture of independence. *Allons, enfants de la patrie.* By tomorrow, Madeleine will be back down off the barricades, and the *ancien régime* will be safe once more."

Staring at Bly, Crosby said, "Come again?"

I explained, "Bly talks in allusions and references. That was the French Revolution that just went by."

With another askance look at Bly, Crosby said, "That wasn't the one with the tea party, was it?"

"No," Bly said.

"Then I wouldn't know it," Crosby said.

"One wishes sometimes," Clement commented, gazing thoughtfully into his brandy glass, "that one actually had Sherlock's powers of observation and deduction."

This connected uncomfortably with my own earlier reflection that I sometimes thought I *did* have Packard's talents and skills; that I knew how to fly a plane, for instance. Not liking this suggestion of an even closer similarity between Clement Hasbrouck and me, I scowled into my drink while he went on, saying, "Think of the many clues to the events around one that are missed day after day."

"Probably just as well they're missed," Crosby suggested, "most of them."

Suddenly dropping into his Charlie Chan persona, his voice becoming more nasal and singsong, his fingertips tapping together to indicate scholarly thought, Fred Li said, "The observed life is like instant replay of a fumble: repeated pain, but no chance of improvement."

With a burst of surprised laughter, Bly looked at the round-faced Chinaman in new respect: "That's wonderful! Did you make that up? That's too modern to be Earl Derr Biggers."

"He's got a million of them," Crosby said sardonically.

"At last count," Fred added.

Clement, still solemn, said, "Interesting, really, the different investigative methods of the different detectives. Sherlock, for instance, is concerned almost exclusively in the verifiable details of the physical world, be it Turkish tobacco or the dog that fails to bark in the night. Your Charlie, on the other hand, is much more interested in character and interpersonal relationships."

"And timetables," Fred commented, grinning.

Crosby pointed a stern finger at Clement, saying, "At precisely two-seventeen, the butler saw you on the stairs to Professor Poopnose's study."

"Well, yes, of course," Clement agreed, nodding, still taking it all very seriously. "There are the conventions of the form to be accommodated. But Charlie's *interest* is always in the goings-on between people, while Sherlock's interest lies in the hard and confirmable facts of the concrete world." Considering his own remark and approving of it, he went on. "I must say that, temperamentally, I find myself more suited to Sherlock's approach. A fortunate thing for the characterization, one supposes."

Bly said, "You don't believe personality and character are important?" I could tell she was thinking about her own work, writting sitcoms, where established character *schtick,* the little recognizable quirks and tics the audience has learned to expect, that gags can be hung on, is all.

But Clement shook his head at her, almost sadly, saying, "I'm afraid, dear lady, I must concur with the Bard, that the soul of man—and woman, of course—must remain forever unknowable."

"Not to Charlie Chan," Fred said, and dropped into that character again. "The soul of man is like the fish in the ice chest; bring it out, and soon it will tell you if it is good or bad."

Bly said, "Miss Marple works from character too."

"And timetables," Fred told her, grinning.

"Character and timetables," Bly agreed.

Turning to me, Clement said, "Which would you say is Jack's main pursuit?"

For just a second, I had no idea who he was talking about. The television series that made me what I am today—rich, famous, and unemployable—was named PACKARD, the character I played was Jack Packard, but I've always thought of both show and lead by that last name. The idea of calling the character "Jack" had never even occurred to me, and, in fact, now that it had been suggested, I found it distasteful. Maybe that merely meant I truthfully didn't want to get to know the damn character that well; we were close enough as it was. I certainly didn't want to cozy up to Jack Packard the way Clement Hasbrouck had cozied up to his beloved Sherlock.

While I was still doping out the question, Bly provided the answer, telling Clement, "Packard came pretty close to combining the two, when you think about it. He was always interested in character—"

"And timetables," Fred said.

"And timetables," Bly agreed, grinning at him. Turning back to Clement, she said, "But he was presented as a kind of Philo Vance character, too, a criminologist who knew a lot about forensic medicine."

"But not much about Turkish tobaccos," I said, feeling the obscure need to defend Packard from being made to seem unnecessarily foolish.

"Different styles," Clement said. "Different approaches, different philosophies of the art of detection. One wonders how they would compare in real life."

"Well, you've already got your murder," Crosby told him, as though it were the most casual thing in the world.

Nobody followed her on that one. Frowning, Clement said, "Do you mean Harriet and Daphne?"

"No, I mean violent death." Crosby gestured at the windows, and the night and the storm beyond. "The pilot," she said.

"Dear lady!" Clement cried in appalled surprise. "That was an accident! Horrid, unforgettably horrid, but an accident."

"Was it?" Crosby grinned around at us, standing there with the rest of us all seated, taking the stage as she would in Las Vegas, enjoying herself. "Isn't that the way the mystery stories work?" she asked us. "With a really tricky murder to dope out? A locked room, or something impossible, or something made to look like an accident."

I said, "Crosby, nobody arranged that storm."

"Nobody had to," she told me. "All you had to arrange was the plane. Everybody had to climb over the pilot's seat to get in and out of it, isn't that right?"

We agreed that was right.

"So there's your opportunity," she said. "Nine of us

flew out in that plane today, us four in the morning, you five this afternoon. Everybody but Danny and Mort and George. Somebody with a little knowledge of airplanes could fix something, screw something up while they're climbing out of the plane. Then the pilot takes off, the storm makes him turn back, instead of him crashing out in the middle of the ocean somewhere, it happens here, and we all blame it on the storm. So that's the method. There we are, opportunity and method already. So all that leaves is motive. Right, Fred?''

"And the timetable," Fred told her.

"But none of us knew the man before today," Clement objected.

"Are you sure about that?" Crosby asked him. "Are you sure there isn't some secret in somebody's past, one of us here, and that person saw the pilot and said, 'Uh-oh, he knows I'm really Three-Fingered Louie and an escaped con from Alcatraz. I better get him before he recognizes me.' So there's your motive, and all you guys have to do is work out the details. Which of us is Three-Fingered Louie?''

"None of us," I told her, half going along with the gag and half bothered by it. "I may not be much of a detective," I went on, "but I have noticed that every one of us has five fingers on each hand."

"Full fathom five," Bly said with such gloom that I looked over at her in surprise, seeing her gaze with a very troubled air toward the windows.

I said, "Bly? What is it?"

"I don't like this game," she said. "I'm sorry, Crosby, I know it's just for fun, but I don't like it."

Crosby, looking abashed, and looking like someone who isn't used to being abashed, said, "Not funny, huh? The man's really dead, is that what you mean?''

''I don't like thinking about him down there,'' Bly said, putting her arms around herself, hugging herself. ''Still jammed inside that little fuselage, down there in the black and the cold and the wet.'' She looked at me, and I could tell she was embarrassed to feel like this, but couldn't help it. ''The water doesn't roil around so much down at the bottom, does it?'' she asked.

Bly's great strength, in her work and in her life, is her imagination, but sometimes imagination can turn around and bite you. ''It's very calm at the bottom,'' I assured her. ''And he isn't feeling anything anymore.''

''I keep remembering Shelley Winters,'' she said, ''in *Night of the Hunter,* dead at the bottom of the river in that car, with the current making her long blond hair sweep out behind.''

''Jesus,'' Crosby said, shivering, ''I'm sorry I started this.''

''You and everybody else, baby,'' Fred told her.

Getting to my feet, I said, ''Maybe today's over. Come on, Bly, say good night.''

''All right.'' She rose, and smiled a bit shakily at everybody, saying, ''Good night, Gracie. I'm sorry I was morbid. It just came over me.''

''I went too far,'' Crosby said, ''and I'm sorry. The same kind of thing happened to me once or twice before.''

''Once or twice a day, you mean,'' Fred told her, also standing. ''Come on, kid, you've had a busy day.''

''Macho man,'' Crosby told him, and said to Bly, ''Don't pay any attention to me, that's the best way to handle it. I get a little dumb idea, and I run with it.''

With a mocking look at Fred, she said, "Or a big round dumb idea, and hang out with *that*."

"Still . . ." Clement said, slow and thoughtful, and when we looked at him, he was bent forward in his seat, brandy glass cupped in both hands as he frowned with great intensity at the windows.

Fred said, "Clement? You don't take this bubblehead seriously, do you?"

"Thanks a lot," Crosby said.

Clement seemed to wake from a deep sleep. Looking around at us all on our feet, he said, "What? Oh, no, of course it was just a game, I realize that."

"You coming upstairs?" Fred asked him.

"Soon. Soon."

So we all said our good nights, and Fred and Crosby and Bly and I left for the guest tower. Looking back from the observation room doorway, I saw Clement leaning forward in the chair, staring again at the window, drink forgotten in his hand.

By golly, he *did* look like Sherlock Holmes.

7

The scream woke me out of a sound sleep. At first I was disoriented, knowing only I was in a strange bed in a strange room in almost total black darkness, relieved only by the indirect faint amber glow of the night-light in the bathroom, showing as a tall thin rectangle of muted orange-rose defining the slightly open bathroom door. I sat up, trying to figure out where I was, what was going on, what had awakened me, and beside me Bly rolled over and said, "Sam? Whazzat?"

"Bly," I said. So that was all right.

There were shuffling noises outside; and memory was returning. Also basic knowledge, such as that there's a light somewhere near to hand beside every guest-room bed. I reached out blindly beside me, pawing the air, felt a lampshade, groped for the base, slid my fingers up it, found the switch, and jolted the room into existence with incredibly harsh white light. Beside me, Bly groaned loudly and dragged the covers over her head.

Someone was moving around outside. "Wait here," I

told Bly unnecessarily—she was making no move at all toward getting up—and got out of bed. Shrugging into robe and slippers, I crossed the room, opened the door to the vestibule, and found Fred Li out there, just switching on the lights. He, too, was in robe and slippers, though his crimson dressing gown with the writhing dragons on the back was considerably more exciting than my basic black number. When he turned around to look at me, there was a small pistol in his hand. "Hello," he said.

"Hello," I said, and pointed at the gun. "What do you plan to do with that?"

He looked at it, considering my question. "Wave it around mostly, I suppose," he said, "since it isn't loaded."

I sensed movement at the foot of the stairs, in the guest parlor. "Something happened," I said. "We should go see what it is."

"You're right." Holding the pistol pointed vaguely at the floor, he squinted up at me and said, "You know? I'm realizing that tall blond giants dressed all in black make me nervous."

"Short round Chinamen with guns in their hands do the same for me," I told him. "No matter which of you isn't loaded. Come on."

Having dealt with our xenophobia, we hurried down the stairs to the guest parlor, where we found Harriet Fitzgerald, in voluminous pale-striped flannel pajamas, in a state of collapse on one of the sofas facing the useless fireplace. Betsy Hasbrouck, seated beside her and wearing a frilly pink wrapper, held Harriet's hand and murmured to her, though Harriet seemed unaware of her presence. When I moved closer, Harriet's eyes were glazed, out of focus, as though she'd taken some strong tranquilizer.

The only other person in the room was Jack French, fully dressed, pacing back and forth, hands clasped behind his back like an impression of Napoleon the night before going into battle. Jack's mouth kept twitching, pulled back into a tense grin, and he flashed looks this way and that as he paced, never quite meeting anybody's eye.

Still, he seemed the best bet to tell us what was going on, since Harriet was obviously out of it and Betsy had her hands full as it was. I turned toward Jack, about to intercept him on his nervous trajectory, when I saw Mort Weinstein in one of the guest-room doorways, gesturing at me. Mort's hairy-bear face looked very solemn, and he was hurriedly dressed in slacks, pullover sweater, and slippers. The room behind him, I remembered, was the one that had been given to Harriet.

Fred and I crossed over there, leaving Jack French to pace, Harriet to collapse, Betsy to soothe as best she could, and Mort said to us quietly, "Come in here, will you?"

We would. Mort shut the door as I looked across a room very similar to mine upstairs. In the open bathroom doorway, in striped blue and white pajamas and a maroon smoking jacket with velvet collar, Clement Hasbrouck stood, hands in jacket pockets. His long face was glum, even grim. I said, "What is it?"

Mort said, "Harriet wanted to talk to Daphne, and—"

Fred Li, who had put his empty pistol away in his robe pocket, said, "What time is it anyway?"

"Ten to three," Mort told him. "Half an hour ago, Harriet woke up and decided it was a good time to talk to Daphne, work out their troubles. She went out to the hall and knocked on Daphne's door, but there wasn't any answer. She tried the door, and it was locked. So she came back in here to go through the bathroom. These two rooms share that bath.''

We had individual bathrooms upstairs. I said, ''Is it the same on the other side of the parlor?''

''Yes,'' Mort said.

The idea of the Hasbroucks and Jack French sharing a bathroom might have been comic under other circumstances, but not with all these troubled faces around us. I said, ''Okay. Then what?''

''This door was also locked,'' Mort said, gesturing at the bathroom door, which now stood open. ''I just forced it myself.''

''Forced it?'' Now I realized there were a hammer and large screwdriver on the bed. ''Mort,'' I said, ''what's happened here?''

''Harriet heard water running in there,'' Mort explained, as Fred crossed to look through the bathroom doorway. ''She knocked, called Daphne's name, got no answer. Finally she got scared, and came around to my room, and asked if I had a key. But the bathroom door was bolted on the inside, and the key to the bedroom door was in the lock, on the inside.''

Across the way, Fred turned back from the doorway. He looked as though he might be sick. While Clement watched him, nodding gloomily, Fred put out a hand to the wall to support himself.

Mort said, ''So I forced the door.''

I knew I'd have to go over there and look, but I didn't want to. I said, ''She's definitely dead, is she?'' Hearing how stupid that question was, I said, ''Excuse me,'' which was also ridiculous, and went over to look in at Daphne Wheeler, in the tub full of rose-colored water. Wrists slit, but blood no longer pumping out. Someone had turned off the faucets, so the water in the tub would be cooling now, along with the body. The knees, breasts, shoulders, and head, emerging from the red water, looked shrunken, shriveled, and dead-white.

No wonder Harriet had screamed, no wonder she was now in such a state of collapse and shock. Daphne had taken the rejection seriously, had thought her own bad behavior at dinner had really been the last straw, had not waited for the rapprochement Harriet had known was next on the agenda. "Poor Harriet," I murmured, looking at the body. "How could she guess Daphne would believe her?"

Behind me, Clement said, "Oh, my dear Sam, no. I'm sorry, but don't you see what this is?"

I looked at him, where he frowned almost caressingly at Daphne. "It's suicide," I said.

"No, Sam. When I tell you my reasoning, you'll have no choice but to agree." He nodded in gloomy satisfaction at the corpse. "I am very much afraid that what we have here," he said in his rich voice, "is murder."

8

"I know it sounds melodramatic," Clement went on, "but you'll see—"

"It sounds ridiculous," I told him. I didn't like being awakened in the middle of the night for *this,* and then have to put up with Clement Hasbrouck emoting all over the place as well. I said, "The woman was drunk. She was miserably unhappy, she'd just made a fool of herself in public, she'd been rejected and turned out by Harriet, she felt she had no place to go, no sense of worth, she was undoubtedly feeling very sorry for herself, and this is what happened. It happens all the time. The woman committed suicide."

But Clement shook his shaggy head, saying, "You are talking in terms of character, motivation. I am talking only about observable facts. Come see for yourself."

He passed me, going into the bathroom, and I followed. It was a long and fairly narrow room, with the tub and toilet on the left, two sinks and a long makeup mirror on the right, doors at both ends. Harriet's and

Daphne's toiletries were scattered around both sinks. Next to the tub, a clear plastic shower curtain was pulled back to the wall and gathered with a thin loop of brass chain. The fan that automatically turned on when the light was lit hummed discreetly. One brown fleece-lined slipper stood on the tile floor. Clement pointed at it, saying, "A small matter. She would have worn two slippers in here, or none."

"She was distraught," I said. Behind me, Mort and Fred Li had come to the doorway and were watching and listening.

"As I said," Clement told me, shrugging it off, "a small matter. As is the fact that the other door was unlocked." He pointed to it.

"She had the bedroom door locked," I said. "She knew no one could get at her."

He gave me the thinnest of smiles. "I thought she was distraught," he said. "Oh, well, no matter. The only point is, these bathroom doors, as you have no doubt noticed yourself, can be locked only—bolted, actually—from the inside."

I hadn't noticed, but I was willing to take his word for it. "All right," I said.

"As to the bedroom door being locked from the inside," Clement said with just a hint of scorn in his manner, "with the key conveniently left turned in the lock so no other key could be inserted from outside, surely, Sam, everyone in this building has been around locked-room murder stories often enough to be able to arrange that with no trouble at all. As just one example, a pair of tweezers such as any one of us might carry in our toilet kits can be put into the keyhole from *outside* the door, once the murderer exits, with the door unlocked but the key in place. With the tweezers, the key is turned, locking the door."

"I've heard of that method in fiction," I admitted, "but I don't know if it's ever been done in fact."

"In due time," he said, "we shall look at that bedroom key to see if it might show new scratches where it was gripped by the tweezers. But I expect other indications as well. I haven't been in Miss Wheeler's bedroom as yet, but when we do go in there, I believe we will find that the bed has not been slept in, but the covers will be disarranged as though someone had slept *atop* them. Miss Wheeler's nightclothes will be on or near the bed, and so will the missing slipper. And one pillow will wear a fresh pillowcase."

Sounding annoyed, Fred Li said, "Clement, what the fuck is the matter with you? Are you doing Sherlock Holmes?"

Clement gave him a mild look. "I would never offer myself in comparison to the master," he said. "Still, over the years of association, one does develop certain habits of mind, habits of observation."

"Clement," I said, "you're going to have to do better than this. So far, all you're doing is some sort of joke in truly bad taste."

"Sam, please," he said, giving me a hurt look. "I had thought we understood each other. I had thought you would realize I take my position much more seriously than that."

"Position?" I asked him. "What position?"

Quietly, from behind me, Mort said, "He's getting a new series."

I turned to frown at Mort. "What?"

"A new Sherlock Holmes series," he said. "On

ABC. An eight o'clock half hour, for the kids. The network figures the video games and all that have brought up a whole new generation of kids who know Sherlock Holmes and can get into the puzzles and all.''

I looked back at Clement. ''Well, congratulations,'' I said. ''But I don't see where that connects with anything.''

Clement couldn't help a faint smile; thinking about his new series, no doubt. He said, ''There have been those who have called me Clement Hasbeen; oh, yes, there are, I know it. One drunk at a party in the Valley not long ago asked me why I didn't apply for admission to Madame Tussaud's. I had begun to fear that I was, well, that it was, that Sherlock had finally ceased to be of interest in this world. But *now*—Sam, I promise you, I will go to any length not to make a fool of either Sherlock or myself. Which is why I was so hesitant to mention the matter at all, once I saw the proof that this was a case of murder. But if no one else were to notice it . . .'' He shrugged. ''We do have a duty,'' he said.

''Noticed what?'' I demanded. ''One slipper? An unlocked door?''

Speaking exactly as though he were giving the title of the short story in which Dr. Watson would recount this adventure, simultaneously pointing dramatically at the object he meant, Clement announced in his rich baritone, ''The feather in the bathtub.''

9

Now what?

It was murder, all right, Clement was absolutely correct. He had seen the small curved dark feather floating in the rose-red water in the tub, and had known immediately what it meant, I'll give him credit for that, even before bending close to the dead woman's face to see the faint bruises on her mouth and cheeks. He had known that Daphne Wheeler had been murdered, that the murderer had tried to make it look like suicide, but that in his—or her—haste, one or two small mistakes had been made. The slipper, the unlocked door, even the condition of Daphne's bedroom when we entered it, all might easily have been glossed over and missed in the shock of her death and the natural assumption that it was self-inflicted. But the feather changed all that.

The fact is, foam rubber rots in the Caribbean, and that's why all the beds in this house on Munro's Island were furnished with feather pillows. Knowing that, we all saw immediately what had happened, and when we opened the connecting door and went into Daphne's bedroom, the evidence was there to prove it.

Daphne had not locked herself in. Drunk, unhappy, exhausted, she had been led here from dinner by Betsy Hasbrouck, who had helped her out of her clothes and into her bulky flannel nightgown and fleece-lined brown slippers. Betsy had then stayed with her, talking, trying to find some way to lift Daphne out of the slough of despair and self-hatred in which she was hopelessly floundering. (Daphne had, in fact, mumbled vaguely about suicide during that time.)

The death of Ralph McCloskey, the pilot, was also bothering Daphne, making her frightenedly aware of just how unimportant any one of us can become, if luck is against us. Her own misery and McCloskey's death were somehow all mixed together in her head.

In any event, Betsy didn't leave her until Clement came upstairs, shortly after the rest of us. Then she said good night to Daphne, told her again to try to sleep, and went with Clement into their own room and to bed, only to be awakened hours later, when Harriet screamed. That was when Mort had pried open the locked bathroom door and Harriet had looked in to see Daphne dead.

This is what had been happening in the meantime: Daphne, worn out, had finally climbed on top of the bed, not getting between the sheets, not even taking off her slippers. She had fallen asleep at last, probably on her back. Then, sometime later, the killer came into the room. He—or she, the whole thing could have been done just as well by a woman—took one of the pillows from the bed and pressed it down over Daphne's face, suffocating her, not long enough to kill, but long enough to knock her out. In Daphne's struggles, before losing consciousness, she had bitten the pillow, biting through the cloth, which is how she got the feather in her mouth or between her lips.

The killer hadn't noticed. He—or she—had seen only the rips in the pillow and pillowcase. There was clean linen in the bottom drawer of a dresser in each guest room; the killer took out a fresh pillowcase and put it on the pillow, folding the torn one neatly and putting it under all the other linen in the drawer.

Next, the killer pulled off Daphne's nightgown, rolled her off the bed onto the floor, and dragged her into the bathroom, locking the bathroom door on Harriet's side so as not to be disturbed. One of Daphne's slippers had come off near the bed, as Clement had suggested, but the other had stayed on till the bathroom. The killer had struggled Daphne into the tub and started the water, and then had broken open a disposable razor from Daphne's toilet kit, using the blade to slit Daphne's wrists, and even including a few shallow extra cuts on the left wrist, as though Daphne had been building up her courage to do the job.

After that, the killer had probably waited long enough to be sure Daphne was really dead, or definitely dying, before leaving, not having noticed the small feather fall from Daphne's mouth into the water. Using the tweezers trick Clement had mentioned—or maybe some similar trick—the killer had locked Daphne's bedroom door from the outside, presenting us with a classic locked-room mystery, and had then presumably gone back to his—or her—room.

Here's the physical evidence we had to verify that reconstruction of events. We had Betsy's description of her evening with Daphne, including the fact that when she left for the night, Daphne was on her feet but no more than half awake, and that the bedroom door wasn't at that time locked by Daphne. We had the small rip in the pillow, and the torn and neatly folded pillowcase in the bottom dresser drawer. It was the slipper in the bathroom that had suggested to Clement that Daphne had been asleep on top of the bedcovers, still wearing her slippers, when she was attacked. There were no visible scratches or marks on the bedroom door key, but we had so much else that it hardly mattered, including a pair of faint scuff lines in the carpet leading from the bed to the bathroom doorway, showing where Daphne had been dragged.

There was to be no more sleep for anyone tonight, of course, with the possible exception of Jack French, who retreated back into his own room once he found out what was going on and that it had no apparent direct bearing on him. But the rest of us were up to stay. Danny went off to radio the news to Puerto Rico, feeling this thing should be reported as soon as possible even though, with the storm outside, there was nothing anyone could do about it. After that, he and Crosby went to the kitchen to start an early breakfast.

Meantime, Mort and George set themselves the job of getting Daphne out of the tub and wrapped in a spare blanket and carried down to one of the freezers below. Bly joined Betsy in trying to soothe Harriet, who simply refused to believe it was murder no matter what anybody said; Harriet remained convinced it was suicide, and blamed herself completely. And Clement and Fred and I went to the observation room to talk things over and see what should happen next.

"I must apologize," Clement told us once we three had sat down together. "I'm afraid I was overly theatrical in presenting the situation upstairs. I can only plead the habits of a lifetime."

Fred said, "I'm getting to like your habits, Clement, don't apologize for them. You're the only one of us who was going to see Daphne's death wasn't suicide."

Clement was pleased, but did his best to display modesty, saying, "Of course, what I did was merely the beginning. The real work starts now."

To our left, out the observation room windows, dawn was appearing, an angry gray smudge along the horizon, with the raging clouds dimly to be seen, swirling above. It was becoming tomorrow, and unreality had well and truly set in. "You mean," I said to Clement, "who did it."

"Of course."

Dropping into his Charlie Chan act, singsong voice and tapping fingertips, Fred said, "Where is murder, is always murderer."

"That's where it breaks down," I said. "All right, we saw the evidence, we know it's true, she didn't kill herself, someone else did. But Daphne Wheeler? Why *her*? There's only eleven of us here. I don't know about you two, but I never even met Daphne Wheeler before yesterday."

"Same here," Fred said.

Clement nodded. "The difficulty perhaps contains its own solution," he said.

Fred gave him a sharp look, saying, "That sounds like one of mine."

"I do beg your pardon," Clement told him, allowing himself a small smile. The situation was serious, and yet none of us could entirely deny the comic element. Clement went on. "I, too, had no prior knowledge of Daphne Wheeler, nor, I am sure, had my wife, Betsy. I presume you can say the same for your ladies." When we both agreed, he said, "The manservant George would not be expected to travel in circles similar to Miss Wheeler's."

I said, "Jack French sure *seemed* to be meeting Daphne for the first time yesterday at the plane."

"Fine," Clement said. "So that leaves our hosts, both of whom might have met Miss Wheeler socially prior to this, but would be extremely unlikely to have any sort of relationship with her that could lead to a barbarity like this. The motives for murder, after all, are but three: greed, fear, and rage."

"And insanity," I said.

He nodded, but told me, "I include that within rage. In any event, none of the three motives would seem to have any bearing on our hosts. When everyone else, therefore, has been eliminated . . ." He shrugged his hands.

I said, "No, Clement, not Harriet. Look how she's taking this."

"Oh, really, Sam," he said. "Harriet is not merely the embodiment of Miss Marple, you know. Harriet is an *actress*. You may not know this, but she is RADA trained. She had a long and distinguished stage career, with some film work as well. Miss Marple is a kind of retirement for her, an annuity to take her through her old age."

I said, "There's acting, and then there's acting. I can chew a piece of scenery a bit myself."

"We all can," Fred said. "I did a Japanese prisoner-of-war camp commander on television a few years ago that has some people *still* scared to turn the lights out when they go to bed."

"All right," I said. "And there's no doubt in my mind Harriet is really and truly in a state of shock. You can't *act* ice-cold hands and depressions under the eyes."

"Her being in a state of shock," Clement said, "in no way contradicts the idea that she is a woman who, in a fit of rage, has just committed the first murder of her life."

Fred said, "The problem with all that is, Harriet didn't have to kill Daphne to get rid of her. All she had to do was point at the door and say *go*."

"As she'd done," I pointed out.

"Ah, but could she?" Clement asked. "Daphne, it seems to me, was making some very obscure threats during that unfortunate scene in the dining room. If people *knew*, she said, if they knew the real Harriet, or if they knew what Daphne knew about Harriet, something along those lines. Very vague, but clearly threats."

"I didn't hear it that way at all," Fred said. "It sounded to me just like a drunk talking like a drunk. If Harriet's fans knew she was a dyke, or knew how mean she was to Daphne, something like that. Self-pity." Grinning at us, Fred shrugged and said, "I get like that myself sometimes. Ask Crosby."

"Either interpretation is possible," Clement agreed. "For the moment, let us assume my interpretation is the correct one, and Harriet could not, or dared not, rid herself of Daphne quite so easily as it might have appeared."

"Clement," I said, "you may be right, but I for one don't buy it. And in any event, it isn't up to us. The whole thing can be turned over to the police as soon as the storm lets up.''

Clement cocked an eyebrow at the windows. Beyond, the day was a bit more clear, the horizon an angry glaring gray and white, the sky filled with tumbling dark clouds, the sea all around our little island whipped and foaming. ''That may be some time yet,'' he said.

''In the meanwhile,'' I told him, ''nobody's going to get away from this island. So there's no point accusing Harriet of anything, or locking her up, or anything like that.''

''Oh, certainly not, I quite agree.'' Clement smiled and nodded, leaning back in his chair, including us both in his glance as he said, ''Beyond which, of course, I am not entirely satisfied by the theory of Harriet's guilt myself. That's why I began this discussion by saying that most of our work was still in front of us.''

''Wait a minute,'' I said, with the feeling I'd lost my place somehow. ''You've just been arguing that Harriet *is* the killer.''

''Of course.'' He spread his hands as though everything were crystal clear. ''One tests the hypothesis, puts it up against the strongest possible arguments. Harriet is certainly the most obvious, and so far the only logical murderer. But how certain can we be? Only when we have assured ourselves absolutely that no other member of our party had any relationship with Daphne Wheeler that could have led to her death will we be able to say that the most obvious solution is indeed the true one.''

Fred said, ''Eliminate the impossible. Whatever's left, however unlikely, is the truth. That's one of yours.''

With his little thin-lipped smile, Clement bowed his head and said, ''I recognized it.''

I said, "Clement, are you seriously suggesting we play detective?"

He looked at me with feigned surprise. "But, Sam," he said. "Of course. That's what we *do*."

10

The strange thing was, everybody else seemed to think it was a good idea except Jack French, who didn't think *anything* was a good idea, and Harriet, who didn't come down to breakfast and thus didn't hear the discussion. Danny Douglas, who was apparently one of those people who get through life with the help of a whole lot of pills of different kinds, had dipped into his "feelgood" supply and dosed Harriet with enough tranquilizers and downers to keep her asleep for most of the day. The rest of us sat around the same table where we'd had dinner the night before and, the time not yet five in the morning, we ate the breakfast of scrambled eggs, bacon, toast, orange juice, and coffee that Danny and Crosby had put together.

It was during breakfast that Clement presented his scheme, saying, "As Fred put it very succinctly a little while ago, wherever there is a murder, there must of necessity be a murderer. Someone in this house did that beastly thing to Daphne. None of us would prefer to believe that it was done by Harriet—''

''Oh, Clement,'' his wife, Betsy, protested, ''it couldn't be! I've spent the last *hour* with poor Harriet. She loved Daphne, I have to say that. I'm not so certain she'll ever recover from what's happened here.''

Other people chimed in their agreement, to all of which Clement merely nodded, saying, ''Certainly, it does seem extremely unlikely, but that leaves us only one alternative. If Harriet didn't kill Daphne Wheeler, then someone at this table *did*.''

That stopped everybody in their tracks. People stared around at all the other staring faces, and gradually it did sink in: There had been a murder. There must therefore be a murderer. No one else was on this island but those of us gathered around this table, plus Harriet Fitzgerald, unconscious upstairs. Someone here had to be the guilty one.

Mort finally broke the stunned silence, saying, ''You're right, Clement, you have to be. And when the police get here—''

''We don't know when that will be,'' Clement pointed out.

Mort said, ''Even if the storm hangs around for two or three days, as it might—''

Crosby's fork hit her plate with a clatter: ''Two or three *days*!''

Danny Douglas told her, ''This is hurricane season, and this part of the ocean is what you could call their staging area. They build up and build up, and eventually head north. So far, this isn't a hurricane; it hasn't built up the momentum, it's just a lot of swirling storm.''

"But two or three days," Crosby protested, looking around. "We have to stay *here,* cooped up together?"

"With one of us," Clement added unhelpfully, "a murderer."

"Clement," Mort said, trying again, "sooner or later the police will get here, maybe even later today—"

"Possible," Danny said doubtfully. "The weather reports, though—" He shook his head.

"What has been bothering me," Clement said, talking directly to Mort but generally to us all, "is the idea that Daphne Wheeler's death might not have been either the beginning or the end."

He had everybody's attention now. Mort said, "Meaning what?"

"I am remembering Miss Tucker's conceit of last night," Clement explained, "about the death of the pilot. She meant it as—"

"That was just a gag!" Crosby said.

"Yes, of course," Clement told her. "I was about to say, you meant it as a joke, but we can now see that the scenario you presented was a distinct possibility. If that is the case, then the murder of Daphne Wheeler was the *second,* not the first, and there's no telling how long the series is intended to go on."

"That's stupid!" Jack French snapped. Until then, he'd merely sat hunched at his place, eating from time to time, sometimes glowering at whoever was speaking, but now he sat up and said, "What the hell are you people up to? Trying to turn this into a mystery story?"

"It is a mystery story," Clement told him.

"*You* aren't a detective," Jack said, pointing his fork at Clement. "You aren't Sherlock Holmes. You're a second-rate *actor*."

"Jack!" Danny said.

"There's a woman dead," Jack insisted. "Her lover killed her, who now can't face what she did. When she wakes up, when the police get here, she'll confess all over the lot. Don't make *mysteries* out of the goddamn thing."

Half the people at the table wanted to dispute Jack one way or another, but it was Danny Douglas's thin clear tenor that broke through, saying with cold disdain, "It was this second-rate actor, Jack, who discovered it was murder in the first place."

While several other people loudly agreed with that, Jack brusquely waved the idea aside, saying, "The police would have seen it, don't worry about that."

Quietly, in a gentle and friendly fashion, Mort said, "Actually, Jack, they wouldn't. By the time any authorities at all could get here, there'd be no more crime scene to study. You agree we couldn't just leave the woman there, where she was."

"All right, all right." Jack made a bad-taste face. "Clement Hasbrouck was brilliant. Finest parlor trick ever seen. But now his stunt is *finished*, dammit. Actors! God spare me! They never know when to get off the stage."

The generality of this attack pretty well silenced the table, until Crosby Tucker brightly turned to Danny and said, "You knew this man in the old days. Was he better as a drunk?"

Jack flashed her a look of ice-cold fury, while Danny looked at first startled, but then grinned and said, "No. He was pretty much like this, really."

"So I guess there's no cure for it," Crosby said.

Jack abruptly stood up, throwing his napkin onto his

half-eaten breakfast. "Go on with your parlor games," he said. "But without me."

Bly, across the table from me, laughed with what sounded like honest amusement. Everybody looked at her in surprise, even Jack, and Bly said to Danny and Mort, "Do you arrange it this way? A dramatic exit from every meal? What hosts you are! Better than Eskimos."

"It just happens," Mort said modestly, while Danny laughed and the tension around the table could be felt to ease.

Except with Jack. "I'll prefer my dramatic exit," he said, "to the melodramatic presence of the rest of you. I'll wait in my room for transportation *off* this rotten island."

As he turned to stomp away, Bly said, "Betsy, are you going to do Virgil with this one too?"

"Oh, no," Betsy said. "This one's on his own." And Jack stalked off toward the stairs.

Tension had been lessened, but not eliminated. For a minute or two after Jack left, conversation was more general. I told Bly how much I'd liked her timely interpolation, and she said, "He shouldn't have made that crack about actors," so then I thanked her for what she'd done, now that I knew she'd been leaping to my defense.

But then the main topic returned, this time brought in by Fred Li, who said, "Excuse me, everybody. We're not really finished here. As Charlie would have said if he'd thought of it"—and he went in and out of his Chan routine—"when danger threatens is not the time to discuss the price of tea."

We all looked at him. Betsy Hasbrouck said, "Danger? What danger?"

"We are stuck on this island," Fred told her, "with a person unknown who has killed at least one time that we know about, and possibly two."

I leaned forward to say, "I'm sorry, Fred, but I just can't believe the business about the plane."

"Still," Clement said in his most sepulchral manner, "Fred is correct to remind us that the possibility exists. And that there are several reasons to believe that the murderer may, if you'll forgive a phrase that would drive Jack French round the bend if he were here, the murderer may strike again. If for no reason other than the fact that we now *know* there was a murder, that the carefully concocted suicide failed of its intent."

Bly said, "You know, when Jack French said that about Daphne having been killed by her lover in a rage, that's when I knew for absolute sure that he was wrong and Harriet isn't the killer. Because that thing wasn't done in a rage, or any kind of high emotion at all. It was cold and planned, Raven without the limp."

Bly tends to be surrounded from time to time by bewildered faces, and here it had happened again. Doubtfully, Mort said to her, "Is that something from Poe?"

I answered for her, mostly because I'm always pleased when I follow that labyrinthine brain of hers. I said, "No, it's Graham Greene. Raven was the professional killer with a limp, the lead character in *This Gun for Hire*."

"Sorry," Bly said. "Those things just slip out."

"When danger threatens," Fred/Charlie singsonged, to bring us back to the subject.

"Right," I said. "If it's all right with everybody, I'd

like us to concentrate, at least for now, on the one thing
we're absolutely sure about, which is the murder of
Daphne Wheeler. Forget the pilot, forget whatever future plans the killer might have. The one thing we're
sure of is Daphne. So the question is, which of us knew
her, to what extent, and what can we put together about
her history and personality? Who *was* she, in other
words?"

Mort said, "Danny and I have known Daphne for, I
guess, seven or eight years. Wouldn't that be about
right, Danny?"

"About that," Danny agreed.

Mort said, "She was a free-lance journalist mostly,
except she hasn't done much of anything the last few
years."

"Since she moved in with Harriet," Danny said.

Mort nodded. "That's right. I think she originally
met Harriet when she went to interview her for some
magazine."

I said, "How long ago would that be?"

"Years," Mort said. "Daphne and Harriet were already together when we first met them."

I said, "You met Daphne through Harriet?"

Mort shook his head, saying, "It was the other way
around, in fact. Daphne did some other writing, too,
short stories, some television work. We hired her to do
a draft of a teleplay. *Two Is a Lonely Number*. Right,
Danny?"

"She seemed right for the job," Danny said. "A
couple of lesbians in a working-class suburb. Nurses.
What happens when the community finds out."

"We lifted it from *The Children's Hour*," Mort said

comfortably. Televison people are remarkably honest about their thefts, if that's the phrase I'm looking for.

"She wasn't very good, though," Danny said. "Lifeless dialogue."

I said, "Did she get a credit?"

"Oh, the project was never done," Danny said. "There were one or two more drafts by a different writer, but the network was always a little afraid of the concept, so it finally just faded away."

"Like so much," Mort said.

I said, "Did you ever hire her again?"

"No," Danny said. "We did option a series idea she had about a cat hospital, but nothing ever came of it."

"Do you know what this book was that she wanted Harriet to help her get published?"

Danny and Mort looked enquiringly at each other and shook their heads.

I said, "When was the last time you saw her, before yesterday?"

"Oh, about two years ago," Danny said.

"Longer than that," Mort told him. "The cat hospital thing was, let me see, the selling season's in February, March . . ."

"Two and a half years, then," Danny said.

"About that," Mort agreed.

I looked around the table. "Did anyone else know Daphne before yesterday?"

"Well, I did, in a way," George said with his soft Caribbean accent.

We all looked at him in surprise. George was, of course, a part of the group, but in a different way from the rest of us. Danny expressed everybody's surprise when he said, "George? Truly? How on earth did you know her?"

"Three years ago," George said, "I was working at the Pink Reef Hotel, you know, on Montego Bay."

"In Jamaica," I said.

Nodding, George said, "That's where I come from, you know. My wife, Blondel, she's there right now, she's having my baby any minute."

"Not exactly any minute, George," Danny told him, and said to the rest of us, "We've been keeping in touch by radio, and Blondel's fine."

Mort said, "But she is due this month."

"A baby born in a hurricane," George said, smiling at us all, "is very strong."

Personally, I thought that was a bit of folk wisdom he'd just made up on the spot. George's expression, whenever I'd glanced at him, was one of quiet amusement, as though he found these actors and TV people a frivolous and silly group on the whole; and maybe he was right. I said. "You met Daphne Wheeler at the Pink Reef Hotel?"

"I was relief bartender," he said, "three nights a week. Some film people were down making a movie around Jamaica. Miss Fitzgerald was—"

"*Death of a Zombie*," Danny said.

"Yes, I think so," George agreed. "They were making the film in Jamaica, but pretending it was Haiti. Miss Wheeler was there, but she was not working on the film. She was, uhhh, at loose ends."

I said, "So she went to the bar a lot."

"Oh, a great deal," George said, smiling broadly. "She told me she was working on a novel."

"Did she say what it was about?"

"Love," George said.

Bly said, "Were Daphne and Harriet getting along well?"

"At times," George told her. "I think Miss Wheeler was bored much of the time. And Miss Fitzgerald was working hard, and was rather impatient."

Danny said, "George? Did Miss Wheeler recognize you yesterday?"

"Oh, no, I don't think so." George smiled. "Miss Wheeler was not one to remember a bartender outside the bar. But Mr. French remembered me, all right."

That got a reaction. Everybody stared, too startled to speak, until Danny Douglas finally found voice. "French?" he asked, and pointed at the empty chair. "*Jack* French?"

"He was there at the same time, at the Pink Reef Hotel," George said, nodding and smiling, as we all gaped at him. I could tell he was having fun outacting the actors. "And he was much in the bar," George added.

I said, "So he and Miss Wheeler knew each other."

"Oh, it seemed so, yes," George said. "They talked together sometimes, crying on one another's shoulder, you know."

Sounding very dubious, Danny said, "Did Jack direct *Death of a Zombie*?"

"No," Mort said, "that was Joe Grubin."

George said, "I believe Mr. French was engaged to an actress in the film, and had come down to be with her, but the relationship was not going well. I don't believe they ever married."

Crosby said, "This is all three years ago?"

George nodded at her. "Approximately so, yes."

Crosby said, "So he was still on the sauce then, in other words."

Mort said, "Jack stopped drinking about a year ago. He was in an automobile accident, a couple of people were hospitalized, one almost died. It wasn't the first time. The judge gave Jack a choice, AA or jail. He took AA, and as I understand it, he's a total believer now."

I said, "I noticed yesterday, he did act like a recent convert, couldn't wait to tell everybody he was an alcoholic."

"Unfortunately," Clement said, "I believe the moment has come when it will be necessary to interview Jack French."

I said, "He won't talk to us."

"But he'll have to," Clement said. "It's in his own best interest to know what the rest of us will be saying to the police, once they arrive."

"If you want to try that on him," I suggested, "don't let me stand in your way."

"Well," Clement said, "what else is there to do?"

"Nothing that I can think of," I told him.

Fred said, "We all have the story till now, and what else is there? I agree with Sam that none of us would get anywhere talking with Jack French. Besides, I don't know about the rest of you, but I didn't get much sleep last night, and this breakfast has just about knocked me out." And he yawned, hugely, in demonstration.

Which caused a series of yawns all around the table, and a general realization that we were *all* weary, now that the excitement was over and the adrenaline surge finished. It was agreed that everybody would retire at least for a few hours, and hope the storm would go away by the time we were ready to face the world again.

Clement announced his determination to beard Jack French in his lair, alone if necessary—he rejected Betsy's offer to join him—and he would let the rest of us know the result.

"I think we'll probably *hear* the result," Fred said.

"I won't," Crosby said, getting to her feet. "In thirty seconds, I'm going to be asleep, and *nothing* will wake me."

So we all left the table, with Danny and George on clean-up detail again, and headed up the stairs for our rooms. Going up, Bly put her hand in mine and grinned up at me, saying, "You take me to the most *interesting* places."

11

It turned out Bly wasn't actually ready for sleep. "Could it really have been Jack French?" she asked, once we were alone together in our room. "God, he's bad-tempered enough."

"In a story," I said, "he'd be the most obvious suspect, and therefore innocent."

"One of the many differences between stories and real life," Bly told me, "and I speak as an expert on both, is that in real life, the guy who looks as though he did it is usually the guy who did it."

"Where's the fun in that?" I asked, as I crawled into bed at last.

Getting in beside me, Bly gave me a knowing grin and said, "You *were* having fun there, weren't you?"

"Oh, God," I said, embarrassed. "Was I? Really?"

"Not as much fun as Clement, though," she said, letting me a bit off the hook.

"Nobody could have as much fun with this as Clement," I said. "The man was born for this scene. But I do have to admit that thing about the feather was a stroke of genius.''

"Which went immediately to his head. And yours, a bit. And Fred's.''

"It's hard not to make a fool of yourself,'' I agreed, "when you're given such a juicy opportunity.''

"I kept waiting,'' she said, "for you to point out you used to *be* a cop.''

"A long time ago,'' I said. "And not much of a cop, even then. Riding around in a patrol car all the time, looking for speeders.''

"There was a bit more to it than that,'' she insisted.

Not much, though. The fact was, I'd drifted into police work the same way I'd later drifted into acting. Being six foot six, I'd gotten a basketball scholarship to an upstate New York college, but then flunked out, went into the army, and was assigned to the MPs only because it was a way to make me available for the regiment basketball team. I was good in basketball, but not quite good enough for the pros, so after the army, with my only training having been the MP duty, I'd wound up on the police force in my hometown, Mineola, east of New York on Long Island. A year and a half of uniformed duty, mostly—as I'd reminded Bly—in a squad car, had ended when a movie was being shot partly in the Mineola neighborhood and an agent "discovered" me. He didn't do much with his discovery, though, and it was only after a couple of pretty lean years out on the Coast that a different agent had put me up for PACKARD, the TV series that changed my life.

But PACKARD had not had much to do with actual police work, and my actual police work had not had much to do with detection, so I didn't see where I could get off by presenting myself as any kind of authority, which I tried to explain to Bly by saying, "If I'd mentioned the thing about being a cop, either people would have thought I was a phony trying to puff myself up, or they would have expected too much from me. Either way, I lose. It's tough enough just avoiding being Packard."

"Well, I'll keep your secret," she said, grinning at me, snuggling very close under the covers. "But only if you'll be very very nice to me for the next half hour."

"I love blackmail," I said.

12

The huge kitchen was down a broad dark passageway behind the dining room, the gray stone of walls and floor inadequately lit by rows of concealed fluorescent lights reflecting from the cream-painted ceiling. For some reason, Sonny Trager had chosen this shadowy area to display his English fox-hunting prints, which Danny and Mort hadn't as yet gotten around to removing. At a little before ten that morning, leaving Bly still asleep up in the room and feeling the need for coffee, I went down this passageway, flanked by dim scenes of leaping brown horses, twisting and fleeing orange foxes, and stiff-looking human beings in red coats, and in the kitchen I found Danny Douglas seated on the center butcher-block island, feet dangling as he read a cookbook, a coffee cup beside him. He didn't see me at first, and I paused to look at this man and to realize how unlikely he was as a successful movie and television producer. He was somehow elfin, seated there with his legs dangling, head bowed as he read the cookbook.

Maybe he should have been a cook, but circumstances led him other ways.

He looked up, saw me, and grinned as I came on into the kitchen. "Well, hello there, Sam," he said, his voice unnaturally loud in the large room.

"Good morning, again."

Putting down his cookbook, hopping lithely off the counter, he said, "You probably want coffee."

"Very much, thank you."

"I have a pot made here," he said, and as he turned away I heard a toilet flush, not far away. I'd noticed that earlier, that bathrooms in this place were not entirely soundproof, probably because of all the stone in the construction. Stone is a very good medium for transporting sound.

"Just one?" Danny asked me. "Or two?"

"One. I'll let Bly sleep as long as she wants."

He gave me coffee, offered cream and sugar—I took cream—and he said, "If we'd known what would happen, eh? This was supposed to be a vacation for everybody, plus a little media exposure."

"We'll be getting quite a bit of media exposure," I suggested, "the way things are going."

"Not what we had in mind," he said with a mock-disgusted shake of the head. "And we got involved in this whole thing only out of friendship. A sort of friendship. And with a very bad man, I may say, a very bad man."

"Oh? Who?"

"Sonny Trager." He laughed at the look of astonishment on my face. "Oh, you didn't know that," he said.

"You and Sonny Trager were friends?"

"In a very strange remote sort of way," he said.

"Sonny liked to hang out with celebrities, you know, stars. He wasn't usually a dealer, a retailer, he was much more important than that, a refiner and an importer. But if you were famous enough, Sonny would make house calls."

I have never been part of the Hollywood drug culture, though, of course, it's always around, like the sea around this island. But I'm too much of a fitness freak to go out of my way to damage my body, so I've never been on the party A list among those people whose main idea of a good time is a sleighride in outer space. I said, "I doubt I ever met him."

"Lucky you," Danny said. "A couple of people on our shows were *good* friends of Sonny's, and it turned out Sonny took a liking to Mort and me, thought we were more stable and reliable than the customers he met us through."

I laughed. "Sonny was on pretty safe ground there."

"If nowhere else," Danny agreed. "That's how we wound up with this goddamn castle, you know."

"I thought you bought it from the government," I said.

"In a way." Danny shook his head at the memory. "It was a very complicated deal," he told me, "and a very hairy one. Sonny was prepared to name names, if it would help him at sentencing time."

"That's normal," I said.

"Yes, it is. Unfortunately, a couple of the names he would have mentioned were people we had, uh, how shall I phrase this?"

"People you were financially close to," I suggested.

He laughed. "That's right."

"Awkward position."

"Well, that's where the deal came in," he said. "If there's one thing in this world that Sonny really loves, it's this house."

"He has odd tastes," I said. "But then, he would have."

"The house was impounded when he was arrested," Danny went on, "and he was afraid something bad would happen to it. It would be torn down, or taken over by somebody who wouldn't, uh, appreciate it. Or turn it into a cheap hotel, something like that. So he offered a very weird deal."

"I can hardly wait."

"If the government would make it possible for us to take over title to Munro's Island and the house," Danny said, "then Sonny would do better than just name names. He would describe trade routes, identify ships and companies, give them almost everything he had. And if Mort and I agreed to take over the place and change it only so far as necessary for our own uses, he would leave off his list of names the people *we* cared about."

"A good deal for everybody," I said, "in a way."

"In a way," Danny agreed. "The government included in the deal that the place would be available for charitable uses, at shared expenses, for the first three years we owned it, which is how you people all got here."

"And when is Sonny due to get out?"

"Never." But then Danny shook his head, and said, "Let me correct that. Theoretically, he could come up for parole in twenty-seven years."

"That's a long time."

"Forever, as far as we're concerned," Danny said. "And in the meantime, Sonny's happy in stir with the idea that his grand house is being taken care of by people who appreciate it and understand it, our company is no longer in danger of losing a couple of very profitable series, and if we ever get through this sudden madness of murder and storms, Munro's Island could be a very enjoyable and profitable investment.''

I sipped coffee, and that nearby toilet flushed again. I said, ''Profitable? You mean you *will* turn it into a hotel?''

''Oh, no,'' Danny said. ''Sonny still has *friends* on the outside, South Americans he didn't rat on or the police can't touch. If we did bad things to Sonny's house, Sonny's friends would do bad things to us.''

A door across the room opened and Clement came out, adjusting his belt. ''Oh, hello,'' he said to me, and gingerly patted his stomach. ''Gippy tummy, I'm afraid.''

''Not surprising,'' I said.

Danny said to Clement, ''Feeling better now?''

''Much. Thank you.''

I said, ''Danny, I don't see any way this place becomes profitable.''

''We can put in screening rooms and production facilities down below,'' he explained, ''in all those storage areas cut out of the rock, where Sonny had his refinery. We can offer the place as an exotic location to shoot, with accommodations for cast and crew, facilities to view the rushes right here, and a well-equipped camera boat so the sea can be used as a second location. The boat's being fitted up in New Orleans right now.''

''And you think you'll get customers?''

''There are two series concepts using Munro's Island being considered by the networks right now,'' he said.

Grinning, he added, "And one of them isn't even by us. We'd be delighted to farm the place out."

"And in prison," I suggested, "Sonny Trager every once in a while will be able to see his house, right there on television."

"He'll love it," Danny said. "He'll tell all the other cons, 'See that? That's *my* place.' " Danny laughed.

Clement, having poured himself a glass of milk at the refrigerator, joined us, saying to me, "You haven't asked me my news."

"News?" I didn't like the sound of that. "Has something else happened?" But Danny would have mentioned anything of importance.

"No, no," Clement said, "my news about Jack French."

"Oh, that's right, you were going to beard him in his lair."

"He was, as you and others had suggested," Clement said, "extremely difficult at first. He wouldn't even open the door. I had to go into our shared bathroom and talk to him through *that* door. I kept pointing out to him that sooner or later the police would arrive, they would interrogate every one of us, and the things most of us would be forced to say about him could very well be considered damaging indeed."

"He couldn't have liked that," I said.

"He disliked it exceedingly," Clement acknowledged, "but finally he saw he had no real choice in the matter, and at that point he unlocked the door and let me in and we had a brief, and I may say not particularly pleasant, discussion. He was not at all forthcoming on any topic, didn't want to tell me what he and Daphne Wheeler had talked about in that bar in Jamaica three years ago, in fact insisted he hadn't recognized George as having been that bartender, though George insists Jack *did* recognize him, and in general was as difficult and prickly as you might imagine.''

''So much for that,'' I said, surprised that the conversation hadn't been even more raucous than Clement was suggesting.

''Well, no,'' Clement said, raising a finger, his eyes glittering. Pausing to sip at his milk, he said, ''It was *not* so much for that. I did at length persuade Jack that for the sake of what all of us would be saying eventually to the police, he should make some sort of effort to get back in everybody's good graces, to explain himself. He finally admitted to me that he had been under strain, that in fact he had backslid twice in the past month or so in connection with his drinking problem, that he had personal and business problems that were weighing on him, and that he felt he didn't have the *time* or the *attention* for what he thought of as a lot of nonsense. Those are almost his exact words.''

''They have his flavor,'' I agreed. ''So he explained himself.''

''To an extent,'' Clement said, and smiled at me, his eyes shining again. I could now see that he was very keyed up, very pleased with himself. Another Clement Hasbrouck triumph must be on the way. ''We finally left it,'' he said, ''that Jack would come down to lunch with the rest of us, that he would then make a statement to us all, and that he would answer any question, within reason, that we might wish to put to him.'' Clement drank more milk and beamed at me, his upper lip white. ''I'm quite delighted,'' he said.

13

Over the course of the rest of the morning, as people reemerged, Clement went on expressing his delight, telling everyone—sometimes more than once—about his successful bearding of the lion in his lair. Only Crosby Tucker, so far as I know, made any attempt at all to take him down a peg or two, saying, "Don't you beard a lion in his *den*?"

"This lion," Clement told her firmly, "was in his lair." So that was that.

After my coffee and my conversation with Danny, I went out to the observation room to see for myself that the storm was no better than ever. A leaden sky, as angry and unhealthy-looking as an old bruise, still swirled with wind. Rain still beat in gusts against the windows, and the ocean was still a frothing mass of black and white. It was probably imagination, but the observation room seemed clammier than before, as though the storm were finally managing to break through our defenses.

It was strange that the storm seemed to have been

with us forever, when it had swept in only around six yesterday afternoon, less than eighteen hours ago. But it was such a mammoth presence, and it held us pinned down here so thoroughly, that it had already taken on the aspect of a normal fact of life: Oh, yes, the storm.

When I first went out to the observation room, George was on the radio, clearly talking to his pregnant wife, beaming at the microphone. To give him privacy, I went down to the other end, where Fred Li joined me, saying, "Any more thoughts about our mystery?"

"Only the old one," I told him. "That I'll be glad when the police get here."

"Listen," he said, sitting forward in his chair, leaning toward me, his round face serious. "Crosby tells me she read a bio on you once, and you were a cop yourself in the old days. Is that so?"

"Traffic cop," I said. "No training in homicide or forensic medicine or anything like that at all."

"Still," he said, "if things got out of hand here, you could always pull rank."

"I don't follow."

"Clement," he said. "Jack French is right; he *is* turning this into a story."

"Yes, he is," I agreed. "But so far he hasn't done any harm, and in fact—"

I broke off because Fred was staring past my shoulder toward the doorway from the living room. I turned around to look, and it was Harriet Fitzgerald coming out, staring straight ahead at the windows and the storm.

There were several people in the observation room at that time, including George still on the radio, Mort and Crosby talking together at the far end, and Betsy near them, knitting something with gray wool and looking out at the storm. Harriet's entrance—and it was an entrance, a professional one, though certainly unconsciously so—drew everybody's immediate attention, and in the abrupt silence George's voice seemed loud as he said, "I better get off now, honey, I'll call you again later. Give baby a pat."

The ravaged but still imperious grande dame, quite different from the fussy Miss Marple portrayal, Harriet looked toward no one, seemed conscious of nothing outside herself. She crossed toward the windows, staring outward, and Betsy rose and hurried toward her, bundling the knitting away in a wooden-handled canvas bag. As Betsy murmured something to Harriet, Bly came in, making much less dramatic an entrance. Looking around, she saw me, and patted the air to tell me to stay where I was, she would join me. I watched Betsy take Harriet in hand, Harriet permitting the other woman to lead her to a small sofa where they could sit together and look out at the storm. Meantime, Bly came over to sit with Fred and me and to say quietly, "Tiptoe."

"What's going on?" I asked her.

"Maybe Ma Joad, maybe Lady Macbeth. Harriet is deciding right now whether or not she can stand it." Glancing over at Harriet and Betsy, and then back at us, she said, "She's on the edge, Harriet, she really is. I was just talking with her upstairs. She could flip out, or she could be strong. It's even money, so far."

Fred said, "Betsy's the one to talk to her, then. Betsy's got a lot of practice at being soothing."

I said, "What does Harriet say today?"

"About the murder?" Bly grimaced and shook her head. "That part she accepts. It isn't suicide, it isn't her fault. That may be what keeps her upright, knowing there's somebody out there who has to be found and punished.''

"Now we have Miss Marple on the case," Fred said.

Bly gave him a look. "I'm sorry," she said, "but that just doesn't strike me funny."

Fred, to my surprise, looked embarrassed. "You're right," he said, and dropped into Charlie. "When the song is out of tune, the singer should sit down."

I said, "I take it Harriet's going to be at lunch."

"Oh, yes," Bly said. "She definitely wants to hear what Jack French has to say. I think she might have a couple questions of her own, too, about Jack and Daphne."

"Also," Fred pointed out, "she'll be more likely than the rest of us to know if Jack is telling the whole truth."

"The two things about the Spanish Inquisition," Bly said. "Surprise, and lunch."

14

The surprise was, Jack didn't show.

With George's help, Danny had put together a lunch of spaghetti primavera and a mixed green salad; two big bowls on the sideboard for everyone to choose from, plus pots of coffee and tea, but no wine. It was a little before one when Danny announced that lunch was ready, and most of us were very prompt. All but one of us, in fact.

That became obvious when everybody had finished serving themselves and chosen seats at the table, and there was one empty place left, to Mort's left, at the foot of the table. (We'd all shifted around since last night's dinner, so I now had Crosby on my left and Bly on my right, and Harriet was over on Mort's right, facing that empty chair.) There was an uneasy moment or two, with people first looking mostly at the empty chair, and then people looking mostly at Clement, who began to fidget and fuss and flash worried looks at the doorway.

It was Mort who broke the uncomfortable silence, in his soft, burring voice, saying gently to the table at large, "It seems one of us is missing."

"He—" Clement said. "There shouldn't be— We agreed—" He looked once more toward the doorway, then abruptly got to his feet. As Betsy, seated next to him, picked up the napkin he hadn't noticed he'd dropped on the floor, Clement said, "I'll just go up and see what . . . Make sure he knows it's lunchtime."

Clement went off. There was absolutely no conversation, everyone taking the opportunity—and excuse—to eat instead. Bending low toward Bly, I murmured, "One word about either Banquo or Elijah, and I blast."

"Actually," she said, "it was Miss Froy I was thinking of."

Betsy, speaking brightly, as though nothing at all odd were happening, said, "This is a delicious spaghetti, Danny. I love these vegetables."

"Oh, well, you know," Danny said, pleased and brushing it off, "it's very easy to make. And the vegetables won't last, they really have to be eaten first."

Other people chimed in with compliments about the meal, which in fact was very good, and that carried us through until Clement returned, alone, looking extremely worried, saying, "There isn't any answer. To be honest, I don't particularly want to go in there by myself. If one or two of you could—"

Fred and I both rose. We joined Clement and headed for the stairs, leaving absolute silence behind us.

When we got up to the guest parlor, Jack's door was not locked, but his room was empty. Fred led the way, me second, a deeply worried Clement bringing up the rear, and we found a fairly messy room but no obvious evidences of foul play. Clement crossed to the interior door, opened it, looked in, and said, "As I left it, just a little while ago."

Fred and I both had a look. It was the bathroom Clement and his wife shared with Jack French, and it was virtually identical to the one across the way where we'd found Daphne Wheeler. This one was empty.

There was an interesting contrast in styles between the personal goods surrounding the two sinks. The Hasbroucks were old troupers, familiar with touring, used to spending weeks sometimes on the road, and the placement of toiletries and cosmetics on their side of the room was neat and compact, ready to be repacked at an instant's notice. On the near side, Jack French had strewn his own goods around as though he'd simply upended a small piece of luggage over the counter. There were many bottles of pills, some prescription. There was also a glass lying on its side next to the sink. I picked it up and sniffed it.

"Booze?" Fred asked me.

"No," I said. "No smell at all. Water, I guess." I stood the glass beside the sink and went back to the bedroom.

"Well," Fred said grimly, "one thing's sure. We've got to find him."

15

On the one hand, we did have to eat lunch anyway, but on the other hand, it was absurd to be sitting there at the table while Jack French was off who knew where doing who knew what. Theories abounded, including Crosby's and Bly's immediate conviction that Jack had also been murdered—but, if so, where was the body?—and Danny's and Harriet's shared belief that Jack himself was the murderer, who knew his scheme had failed and was now hoping to hide until the storm let up enough for him to escape somehow from the island. Clement's theory, more or less backed by Betsy, was that Jack was distraught, possibly drinking, and that whether he was the murderer or not, he had decided the only thing he could do until the authorities came was hide from the rest of us. George's opinion, similar to that but simpler, was that Jack had fallen off the wagon in a big way and was now passed out somewhere in the house; Mort seemed to agree pretty much with that one. Neither Fred nor I offered any idea; I didn't know what

Fred thought about it all, but I myself was coming to the sneaking suspicion that whatever was going on here was more complicated than it had at first seemed.

As we ate, I found my thoughts turning, irrelevantly but amusedly, to Robinson, my majordomo, factotum, and nanny, at home in my house in Bel Air. To think I'd originally considered bringing him along as well! What would *he* have thought of all this? And specifically, what would he have thought of Clement, the two of them being similar in ways neither would have liked pointed out.

Like Clement Hasbrouck, William Robinson is a longtime actor who has always seemed English to American audiences but American to the English. In a way, they were also similar in having found the one part that would carry them through their later years, though in Robinson's case the part—and his use of it—was very different. A man for whom a supercilious expression came as naturally as breathing, Robinson had played snooty butlers and superior valets in movies and on television for decades, playing a sixty-year-old for years and years, until he himself was sixty, by which time changes in the story America tells itself had pretty well eliminated both snooty butlers *and* their feckless employers from the screen. As Robinson's acting career faded away, he more and more filled in the unemployed periods by *being* a butler or valet, hired by stars he'd worked with in films, one of whom had finally passed him on to me. For the last six years he's been in charge of both my houses, and considers himself in charge of me as well. He's not really a butler, of course, he's still *acting* the part, the lovable curmudgeon, sniffing disapproval, the only sane voice in an increasingly mad world.

Robinson here in Sonny Trager's mad castle would make for an intercultural conflict on an epic scale. His dignity would not permit him to take *any* role in these lunatic goings-on; *how* disapproving he would be!

Fortunately, his dignity hadn't permitted him to come along at all, though he hadn't phrased it quite that way. "You surely don't wish to *board* the dogs," he'd said, showing a concern for my boxers, Sugar Ray and Max, that was as touching as it was new. "And someone should be here to maintain the house." Whatever that meant; Robinson never worried about maintaining the Bel Air house when we lived in New York. (Normally, Sugar Ray and Max lived with Bly when I was out of town, the kernel of fact on which Robinson was building.)

The real problem was, Robinson's little rift with Bly hadn't yet entirely healed. Robinson thinks very highly of Bly—she's one of the very few human beings of whom he totally approves—but some months ago she'd made the mistake of casting him in the pilot of a TV series she'd written, and he'd made the mistake of accepting the part, his first in fourteen years. The curmudgeon role was so deep in his bones by now, however, that he couldn't break out of it to save his life, or the part, or the easiness of his friendship with Bly. He had insisted on rewriting the script, objecting to scenes, acting up badly on the set, and finally he'd quit just before he would have been fired.

A chastened Bly, blaming herself for having rashly pulled Robinson from his well-earned—and safe—retirement, had been willing to forgive Robinson, but Robinson wasn't yet sure he wanted forgiveness. He had, after all, suggested only improvements to Bly's little story. The fact that the network hadn't picked up the pilot meant that Robinson would come around soon, feeling vindicated; in the meantime, he was surely right not wanting to travel in close proximity with Bly.

I distracted myself through lunch with thoughts about Robinson, and when lunch was done, the present version of reality returned as Mort organized a search. Both Harriet and Clement announced themselves too emotionally and physically worn to join, so that left eight of us, in pairs. Mort assigned each pair a section of the house, and distributed whatever keys might be necessary along the way from a wooden key rack mounted on the kitchen wall.

Bly and I were given the third tower, the one with the guest rooms the technical people would have used if they'd been able to come out. Fred and Crosby got the basements and storage rooms, Danny and George the central tower containing Danny's and Mort's quarters, and Mort and Betsy took the tower in which the rest of us had rooms. If none of us were successful, then at the end we would all get together to search the main floor. In the meantime, Clement agreed to stay in the main living room, a large baronial space between the dining and observation rooms, from which he would be able to see Jack if, flushed by one of our teams, he tried to move from one section of the house to another. Harriet, who had used all her energies to steel herself for the interview with Jack, was now drained and exhausted, and would go upstairs with Mort and Betsy and, once her room had been searched by those two, she would lock herself in.

Bly and I covered our territory very slowly and carefully and methodically, and we found nothing. This third tower, empty and unused at the moment, was a similar size to the one across the way containing our room, but the individual rooms here were smaller and there was no guest parlor. Every pair of rooms shared a bath. Beds had been made and linens set out in anticipation of the film crew's arrival, which made the place look strangely like a hotel in the off season; particularly with the gray storm rushing past every window.

The only locked room in this tower was George's, which he maintained as a neat but personal space, like a room in a barracks or dormitory. He had brought very little clothing, only a few trousers and shirts and one jacket hanging in the closet. Over the bed were Scotch-taped several Polaroid pictures of a smiling pretty pregnant black girl, frequently on a sunlit beach.

Since every unit of our search area was circular, since, in other words, a person in any bedroom could go through the shared bath to the next bedroom and thus back out to the hall, our search method on all three floors of the tower was that Bly stayed in the hall while I went in and made the circuit. That way, if Jack actually were up here, there was no way he could circle around behind us.

Well, he wasn't. We made our way to the top floor, the smallest in this tapering tower, divided into two rooms and one bath, and we were absolutely alone in this part of the house. From these top-floor windows, the view was spectacular but scary. Far below, the wind-tossed giant waves beat against the rock face on which the house was built, throwing spume high in the air, the rocks and ocean different shades of glaring black, the spray in masses of dirty white, immediately torn apart by the wind. Waves thundered over the beach, waves washed boiling over the small landing strip, burying it. The cloud-filled sky pressed down on our three towers, as though to crush Sonny Trager's silly arrogance to rubble once and for all.

"*Maaassss*ter!" Bly hissed, with a manic cackle. "The *liiight*ning! The *stoooorrrmmm*!"

"There are things man was not meant to know," I told her.

From up here, the architectural follies of Sonny Trager's imagination were more evident. There was this tall tapering tower, echoed by the other across the way, with a third larger tower between us but angled off to the right, to the south, to make a triangle. Between these towers, one looked down at something that resembled more a mountain village than an ordinary house; angled bits of roof, the shingles glistening in the rain, silvery gutters filled with rushing water, small peaks and slants everywhere. Looking down at it, Bly said, "There must be a million places to hide in here."

"Not that many," I said. "Once you're inside, it's a Holiday Inn."

"The Transylvania Holiday Inn," Bly said.

We went back down to the main floor, to find Clement nodding off in the living room, but swearing that no one had gone by him, that we were in fact the first finished. As he was saying so, Danny and George returned to say the central tower was also empty, so we four—with Clement still holding the fort in the living room—went to study the kitchen, lavatory, pantries, and storage rooms at the rear on this level. George and I got up into a lot of crawl spaces, where the sound of the storm *could* be heard and where we both got pretty grubby, but they, too, were empty, and so was everything else back there.

When we finally made our way back to the living room, Mort and Betsy were there, to say the remaining tower was also empty (except for Harriet, locked in her room), and then Fred and Crosby—Fred nearly as dirty as George and me—came back to say the basements, too, did not contain Jack French, dead or alive.

"This is absurd!" Clement burst out. He was getting more and more agitated, as though he expected Jack to leap out from behind a drapery at any second. "The man must be *somewhere!*"

I said to Mort, "What are the ways out of this house?"

"The elevator you came in, that's all. And we shut off the power to that last night, because the line runs outside the house."

"There has to be some other way," I insisted. "What do you do if there's a power failure?"

"In that case," he said, "there's a flight of stairs incorporated into the elevator's track. But nobody's using that today."

"Let's take a look at it anyway."

"Sure," he said, shrugging. "Come along."

Most of us went out to the observation room, following Mort, who explained as he went along, "There's a lot of reasons why it wouldn't be possible that Jack left here by those stairs. In the first place," he said, taking a small lever off a hook on the wall nearby and inserting it in the elevator door, then using it to pull one side of the door open, "with the power off, how's he going to close this door again and get the lever back on the wall?"

"Give us ten minutes," Fred told him, "we'll find a way."

"Okay," Mort said. Stepping into the elevator, he lifted one rear corner of the grooved mat on the floor and flipped it out of the way, saying, "You'll want another ten minutes on how he put the mat back once he was outside the elevator."

We couldn't all fit inside there, not and have Mort do his demonstration. Fred and I stood inside with him, while the others crowded around the doorway, watching. The elevator constantly trembled and one became aware of the moaning and hissing of the wind.

In the floor of the elevator, under the mat, back near the hanging yellow slickers—"None of them missing," Mort informed us—was a square trapdoor. When Mort lifted this, a genie of cold wet air immediately rushed inside and ran around the interior of the elevator.

Noise entered, too, the rushing and howling of big-league winds, the clattering incessant roar of a truly heavy rainstorm. The sound itself was enough to tell you that was no environment for a human being.

Fred and I stepped forward to look down into dizzying space. The elevator's rails, slick and shiny with blown water over oil, angled down a steep slanted face made partly of natural rock and partly of poured concrete. Far below, water surged and humped on the spot where yesterday we had boarded this box. Wind blew, shaking the elevator, whipping up through the open trap. Steep stone-and-concrete steps, with a very low pipe-length railing just on the one side, went down the middle of the track toward the sea.

"The wind would yank you off that," Mort told us,

his baritone clear to us under rather than over the yowl of the storm, "before you got halfway down."

He was right. No one had left this house by that route, and while the storm lasted, no one would leave it. Feeling faint vertigo, I stepped back from the trap, saying to him, "What about the basements? Didn't Trager have a side entrance for cocaine shipments?"

Mort shook his head. "Everything came through here. Security. With only one way in and out, nobody could get in to rob him or kill him. There are drains down there, leading down out of the basements, things like that, but nothing anybody could use as a passage." Looking mildly at Fred, who was still frowning down at the rails and the steps and the storm, Mort said, "Seen enough?"

Fred seemed to rouse from sleep. "Yes," he said, stepping back from the trap.

Mort shut the door, closing out that banshee wailing, and threw the mat back over it, while Clement called from the doorway, "Fred? Sam? Is it really not possible?"

"If he did get out there," I answered him, "he's dead now. And how did he close everything behind himself?"

We three left the elevator, and while Mort pushed its door closed again with that lever, Bly said to Clement, "Here's a good one for you. When you eliminate all the impossibilities and *nothing's* left, then what?"

"I don't agree," Clement told her. He was looking older now, with dark circles under his eyes. His triumphs had turned against him. "Not all the impossibilities have been eliminated, not by any means. For instance, Jack might have been murdered and his killer might have carried his body down here and thrown it through that trapdoor.''

"Well, let's see about that," Bly said, looking around at everybody. "Who was in the observation room this morning, and when?"

With that one simple question, she very quickly established that from the time Clement had last seen and talked with Jack French, there had at all times until lunch been at least one person—and never a solitary person for more than a minute or so—in the observation room, which meant the killer (assuming Jack was dead) would never have had the opportunity to lug his body down from the guest tower, go through the elaborate business of opening the elevator and the trapdoor, throw the body through, and close everything up again without being seen.

"Very well," Clement said, when that was proved, "then here's another possibility. There is not one killer, but two. A partnership, a couple."

I said, "Like Bly and me, you mean."

"Of course," he said, unfazed. "Or Fred and Crosby. Or Danny and George."

"But not," Mort suggested mildly, "your wife and me. We were the other couple doing the searching."

"A pair might have done it," Clement insisted, "and covered their tracks."

I said, "You're assuming Jack is dead. Another possibility is, he's found a hiding place we missed somehow."

"A pair again, then," Clement said. "Careless, rather than guilty."

"If you want to put it like that," I said.

"Jack French was in this building," Clement said. "He cannot have left the building, but he can no longer be found inside the building. What other way can I possibly put it?"

16

So the result was, we searched the house all over again, only this time in a different conformation, and with Clement's active participation. In fact, with Clement's generalship, he organizing who would be where while the search was going on. First, Bly and Betsy were closed in with Harriet, so there couldn't be anything wrong *there*. Then Fred, Crosby, Danny, and George settled themselves in the living room to keep an eye on the major through routes, not to mention keeping the other eye on one another. And then Mort and Clement and I searched the house from top to bottom, and failed to find Jack French.

The only interesting part of it all, aside from Clement's increasing upset and irritation, was the lower rooms of the house, the ones chopped out of the interior rock of the island. I hadn't been down there before, and I knew Bly would be mad with envy, so I kept my eyes open partly so I'd be able to report back what it all looked like.

Which was mad and spooky and grim. There were three levels below the main living area, and only on the top level were there any windows at all, these being two small deepset horizontal rectangles in the large room which once had contained Sonny Trager's armory. An extensive armory, too, from the look of the wooden cabinets still left behind, the guns themselves having been taken away when the government impounded the house. Trager had had racks of shotguns, racks of sub-machine guns, shelves of revolvers and automatic pistols. I said, "Looks like he expected a war."

"He did," Mort said. "His world wasn't just Hollywood parties. At this end, he was dealing with murderers and psychopaths and pirates."

"Pirates," echoed Clement, who was moodily looking out one of the small windows at the storm and the sea. "How romantic."

"Not romantic," Mort told him quietly but firmly, in his burry voice. "In the last twenty-five years, you know, thousands of boats have disappeared in the waters between South America and the States; between, say, Colombia and Florida."

"Bermuda triangle?" Clement asked.

"No. The cocaine smugglers have to keep using new boats that the Coast Guard and Customs don't know yet. So they seize other vessels, private yachts or fishing charters or whatever is fairly small and completely helpless. They pretend to be in distress, they come alongside, they come on board and kill everybody, throw the bodies into the sea, and use that boat for two or three shipments before they sink it somewhere and steal another. Pirates, but not romantic."

"All of that," Clement said, looking away at last

from the window, "to bring drugs into the United States. What a waste."

"Nose candy, they call it in L.A.," Mort said, sounding grim and angry, "as though it came from Santa Claus. People die every day so those clowns can have their little high."

"I blame the law as much as anything," Clement said. "There will always be customers, no matter how hard it gets to find the product. When Sherlock relaxed with cocaine after a difficult case, you know, no one had to be murdered in order to get it to him."

"Quick, Watson, the needle," I quoted.

Clement smiled at me, saying, "Exactly. Harmless in itself, but made harmful by Draconian law."

"That's one way to look at it," Mort said, making it clear it wasn't the way *he* looked at it. But wasn't he surrounded by drugs among his business associates and his stars, didn't he have to turn a blind eye a *lot,* if this is the way he truly felt? I didn't see any point in asking the question, and Mort said, as I looked around, "Are we done in here? There's no place for Jack to hide, dead *or* alive."

I walked over to the window where Clement had been looking out, but it wasn't the view I was interested in. The stone floor had looked different to me there, darker than the rest of the room. Going to one knee, I pressed my palm on the floor and found it cold and wet. "Do these windows leak?" I asked.

Mort and Clement both came over, looking at me curiously. "They never did before," Mort said.

"Can they be opened?"

"Sure," he said. "There's just a little latch on the inside. It pushes out."

I stood and considered the window, which was placed high in the thick stone wall, at just about my eye level; a bit too high for most people. It was one piece of glass, about ten inches high by twenty inches wide, in a narrow gray-metal frame, hinged at the top, with a ratchet arrangement on one side to hold it open as far as you wanted. The view outward and down was of the storm-tossed sea. Upward, the view was of the dark gray concrete underside of the observation room, built out from the front of the house. The latch didn't look as though the window were opened much; it was grimy with dirt, except at the very innermost point, where shiny metal showed, as though the window had been recently opened and closed, and the latch had not been seated as completely afterward as before.

I opened the window. Wind and cold and rain whipped in; the storm had dropped the outside temperature a good thirty degrees from normal, down into the fifties. With the rain and the strong wind, it felt even colder. Leaning close into this blast, I saw that the ratchet kept the window from raising outward more than halfway. There was no possibility that a body could have been pushed through an opening that size. Of course, a chopped-up body could have been disposed of through here, but that's a very messy and time-consuming job, and it inevitably leaves traces.

"Still," I said.

Clement looked at me, bright-eyed as a bird. "Yes?"

"Someone did open the window," I said. "Recently."

Mort said, "Maybe Fred and Crosby, when they were looking down here."

"And left it open for a while?" I put my hand in the way of the wind coming in, and it immediately became

damp, but only damp. "With the window opening outward from the top," I said, "and with the overhang of
the observation room, not that much rain can get in
here, even now. To leave the floor like this, it would
have had to be open a pretty long time."

Clement was frowning around the room, studying the
floor as though something should be there that wasn't.
"This makes no sense," he said.

"We'll ask Fred and Crosby," I told him. "It's
possible they opened the window on their way through,
left it open by mistake, and didn't close it again until
they were going back upstairs."

Clement said, "Why does one open a window? To
pass something in or out. To hear something. To remove a bad smell." He sniffed. "Do you smell
anything?"

"No," I said. "Only wet stone." I closed the window. The latch worked stiffly. Maybe it had been Fred
and Crosby.

From there we went to the upper part of the cocaine
refinery. I say upper part because the refinery was an
open windowless stone space two stories high; at this
upper level, we entered from the arched central hall onto
a metal balcony from which sluices ran down to the vats
below. Cocaine begins as a gluey white paste squeezed
and crushed from the coca plant, then reduced in refin-
eries like this one—though most of them, I think, are
less elaborate than this—to the white powder its fans
know. Some of the more vital elements of this operation
had been either removed or smashed by the federal
agents when they took over the house, but much of the
machinery remained, so when we looked down from the
balcony at the main plant below, what we saw looked

like a mad cross between a moonshiner's still on a grand scale and Frankenstein's laboratory brought up-to-date with lavish grant money. "Bly has to see this," I said. "Before we go, Mort, I have to bring her down here."

"Absolutely," Mort said, grinning his understanding. "No problem."

The metal balcony, three feet wide, ran along only one side of the refinery. A few empty burlap sacks and some other trash lay on it, but nothing else. There was an immediate dizziness if one looked down past one's shoes through the metal grid of the balcony floor; one held tighter to the cold metal-pipe railing. Above, the ceiling was irregularly chipped stone, below, the concrete base of the main house. On the far side, the ceiling angled down so steeply that if this level of floor were continued over there, we'd all have to stoop.

"There's nothing here," Mort said, kicking at a sack. "We've got to clean this stuff out when we get some time. What a pest this place is."

"What if he were wounded?" Clement asked, looking down at the vats and tables.

We looked at him. Mort said, "Jack, you mean?"

"A *failed* murder attempt," Clement said. "Somehow. Jack, wounded, hides away from us all, uncertain which of us tried to take his life."

"I don't see where that gets us," I said. "Alive, dead, wounded, the question still remains: Where is he?"

"Still," Clement said, as I had said about the window. Leaning over the balcony rail, he called at the mad lab below, "Jack!"

"If he *could* answer you," Mort said, "why would he? Let's go down there."

We went down the broad stone staircase, lit, like the passageways upstairs, by indirect fluorescent lighting reflected from the cream-painted ceiling. Again, as with the passageways upstairs, it wasn't quite enough light for the job. At the next level, a large unfurnished stone room into which the stairs emptied had doors in three walls; the one on the right led into the refinery.

That took the longest to search, being full of equipment and cupboards and broken machinery. Mort and I lifted some of the heavier pieces out of the way, he complaining again about not having had the time to finish cleaning the place up. "I'm sorry we've got this damn albatross," he muttered, as we tipped a steel vat and looked inside at a sticky unwashed grubbiness and no more.

"You'll like it better when it's all film labs and screening rooms," I assured him.

"Sure," he said, but he didn't sound convinced.

The rest of the space on that level consisted of several storage rooms, some in use, some not, including the walk-in freezer in which Daphne Wheeler's blanket-wrapped body was being kept, on the floor against the back wall, superstitiously as far as possible from the frozen foods. The most bizarre part of our search must have been when we unrolled the blanket to be certain Daphne was still alone in there; she was. The blanket, stiff as wood, closed reluctantly again around her blue body.

Still finding nothing, we made our way to the lowest level. The stairs were narrower and steeper here, a clamminess exuded from the rock despite all efforts of the baseboard electric heaters, and you really had the feeling now you were descending into the bowels of the earth. Oddly enough, in this narrower space the indirect fluorescents were at last enough light, so this final staircase was the brightest of all.

The bottom level contained the machinery that kept the whole place going. There was the equipment that generated our electricity from the movement of the ocean, the pump bringing up fresh water from the well drilled deep into the island, the hot water heater and water storage tank, the drains and the emergency gasoline generator, should the regular system break down. Beyond these, in the farthest corner, was the dungeon.

That's precisely what it was. A stone cell no more than six feet square, it had a large iron ring embedded in the middle of the floor and three sets of manacles fixed to the rear wall. The door was metal, with a serious lock, and a small square barred opening at eye level. There was no light in the cell, but Mort had brought a flashlight, and we went into this cold room—it had no heat source of its own, and was built into the center of the rock mountain that was Munro's Island, so it was quite cold and dank—and looked around. A four-inch-wide hole in the floor in one corner was the drain. Otherwise, the place was featureless.

"A ghastly place," Clement said. His voice echoed in this hard room.

"I don't know if he ever used it," Mort said. "It was meant for the same people as those guns upstairs. If he were attacked, and there were survivors, and he wanted to know more about the people attacking him, this is where he would keep his prisoners until they felt like telling him what he wanted to know."

"And then he'd kill them," Clement said in his echoing voice.

"Probably so."

I didn't suggest that Bly should see this part. Even her cheerful irony wouldn't hold up to the implications of this room. Had Sonny Trager ever used it? He'd contemplated the idea, built the place, made it ready. That small drain in the corner was the touch that bothered me the most; acknowledging the realities of our shared humanity while planning your organized inhumanity.

This was the end of the trail also for our search. It was impossible that Jack not be here, somewhere here inside this house, alive or dead, and yet he wasn't. Clement, looking like a man whose deepest beliefs had just been shattered—"He *must* be here," he kept saying, "he simply *must* be"—wanted to search again, go back over the territory, not give it up, but there was simply no point in it. There was nowhere else to look. If there was a solution, it had not occurred to any of us, and standing around in this grim and nasty dungeon, where the distant wind made occasional faint moaning sounds in that drain in the corner, wasn't going to help.

"We'll go back upstairs," Mort decided. "There's nothing else to do, Clement," he said at Clement's stricken look. "The search is over. We're finished."

So we left there. We went back upstairs and joined the people in the living room, and that's where we learned about the radio having been destroyed.

17

It was impossible to say just when it had happened. The last time the radio had been used was by George, just before lunch. He'd been talking to his pregnant wife, Blondel, and had cut the conversation short when the strained Harriet had appeared. Since then, we'd had the interrupted lunch and the two fruitless searches for Jack French, so it was impossible to track anyone's movements and say who did or did not have an opportunity alone with the radio. Someone might even have done it while the rest of us were a scant dozen feet away at the elevator, studying its trapdoor and the exterior stairs.

Whoever had done the job either didn't know much about radios or wanted to give that impression, because he or she had smashed it four or five different ways, just to be sure. "It's a goner," Danny said, standing over the dead radio, shaking his head.

"Oh, my poor Blondel," George said woefully.

"Never mind Blondel," Danny snapped at him. "She's all right. *We're* the ones closeted with a madman."

"Mad," Clement said. "Or feigning madness."

It seemed to me that a person who feigned madness by killing other people was likely to be mad anyway, in addition to the pretense, but I didn't see any reason to make the point.

In this last period of time, we'd been gathered into three groups, with no one on his own. While Clement and Mort and I had done the second search of the house, which had taken nearly two hours in all, Bly and Betsy had stayed with Harriet, locked in her room, and were still up there, while Fred and Crosby and Danny and George had waited in the living room. A little while ago, Fred, announcing with a yawn that he wasn't used to the kind of physical activity he'd been going through in the cellars during the first search, had fallen asleep on a sofa in the living room. Not long after that, George had come out here to the observation room to call Blondel again, and had found the radio smashed. He was just back, reporting the news to Danny, when Mort and Clement and I came up from the cellars. Fred slept through it all, with Crosby next to him on the sofa reading a paperback book, but the five others of us went out to look uselessly at the useless radio.

And the uselessness of the destruction is what mainly got to me. "I don't see what he's gained," I said.

"That's why I say he's a madman," Danny told me.

But Clement said, "What he gains is this: No more news will leave this island. No one but us here knows that Jack French has disappeared. Whatever else may happen, no one but the people on this island will be told about it."

Danny's irascibility turned from George to Clement as he said, "How does that change things? We're not isolated forever, the storm will end, planes will come out."

Softly, Mort said, "Clement means only the survivors will give their version of events."

"Exactly," Clement said.

Danny frowned in exasperation. "What are you talking about? He can't kill all of us!"

"That may be, however," Clement said, "what he has in mind."

"Then he *is* crazy," Danny said.

"As we've been saying," Mort told his partner gently.

"I recommend," Clement said sententiously, "we remain in groups henceforward and avoid traveling anywhere in this house on our own."

"Probably a good idea," Mort agreed.

"Then, Clement," I said, "I think you and I ought to go upstairs together to see how Bly and Betsy are getting along."

"You're absolutely right," Clement told me. To the others, he said, "I believe my wife and I will remain in our room until dinner, whenever that may be."

"Seven," Danny told him.

"Maybe a little later," George said.

Mort said, "I'd like to keep some sort of civilized aspect to this thing, if at all possible. Drinks in this room at six?"

We all agreed to that, and Clement and I went on into the living room, where we found Fred more or less sitting up, slumped on the sofa, yawning hugely, and rubbing his mussed-up hair. Seeing us, he grinned sleepily and said, "A group noun has just occurred to me: An athletic suppporter of dicks."

Crosby hit him on the shoulder with her paperback book, saying, "Jesus, Fred, I can't take you anywhere. You're worse asleep than awake."

A muffled version of his Charlie Chan said, "When Morpheus's arms enclose, no man resists."

Getting to her feet, Crosby said, "Come on, Butterball, I'm putting you to bed."

"Again I do not resist," said Fred as Fred.

So the four of us went up into the guest-room tower together, Clement and I stopping at the first level, the amused Crosby and shambling Fred continuing on up to their room while Clement and I crossed the guest parlor and knocked on Harriet's door.

It was Betsy's voice that answered: "Who's there?"

"Clement, my darling," he told her in an unctuous, caring voice. "With Sam."

We heard the key turn in the lock, and then Betsy opened the door, looked out at us, and put her finger to her lips. "Harriet's asleep," she whispered.

Bly appeared behind her, whispering, "At *last* she's asleep. Hi, Sam."

I nodded hello while Betsy whispered, "We'll come around the other way. See you in just a moment." And she closed and relocked the door.

"I wonder what that's about," I said. Clement said nothing, so I suppose for once he had no theory.

In a minute, the door to Daphne's room opened and Bly and Betsy came out, Betsy with a key which she used to lock Daphne's room from the outside, while Bly came over to explain. "Harriet's door's locked from the inside, so she can get out, but nobody can get in at her.''

Betsy said, ''Did you find Jack French?''

''No,'' Clement told her heavily, as though it were his personal fault. ''I simply can't understand it. Much has happened, my dear, very little of it pleasant. Come along, I'll tell you everything.''

We agreed we'd see the Hasbroucks later, and then Bly and I went on up the stairs to the level we shared with Fred and Crosby. Their door was partly open and Crosby was peering around its edge, apparently waiting for us. From the way she stood with the door in the way, she was probably also naked, or nearly so. Behind her, the bed could be seen, full of the mound of Fred Li, a sleepy smile on his face.

''Psst,'' Crosby said.

''Yes?''

''Do me a favor, okay? In case we oversleep, rap on the door at drinks time.''

''Sure,'' Bly said. ''See you then.''

We went on into our own room, and Bly sat on the bed and said, ''You first.''

''You look good there,'' I said.

''Never mind that,'' she said. ''Crosby put the idea in your head, that's all.''

''I've had that idea in my head for years,'' I objected.

''Tell first,'' she said. ''I have tons of gossip for you, but first you have to tell me everything about everything since I saw you last.''

''In that case,'' I said, ''move over and let me sit down.''

18

When I finished, and when Bly finally finished trying to find some theory to explain the disappearance of Jack French—there simply was none, as she ultimately had to admit—she settled down to tell me what *her* news was. With the wild storm still lashing past our bedroom windows, she settled herself comfortably against the headboard, legs crossed tailor-fashion. She *did* look good, but she was being serious now, so I ignored all that, and she said, "Daphne Wheeler and Jack French, first. Remember when we rode out with them on the plane?"

"I remember riding with *him,* believe me, I do."

"Did they act like people who knew each other?"

Considering, remembering, I shook my head. "Not that I saw."

"And yet George says they had long talks together in that bar in Jamaica."

"Three years ago," I pointed out, "for only a week or two."

"All right," Bly said, nodding. "Let me tell you what Harriet says about that. *She* says Daphne did recognize Jack, knew him at once, and her first remark to him, about taking a good stiff drink before you have to fly, was meant to remind him who she was. When he immediately made that curt remark about being an alcoholic—"

"I remember that, too," I said.

"Well, Daphne thought it was meant as a putdown, so she didn't say anything else. She just thought Jack was avoiding her because she reminded him of when he did a lot of drinking. But she was sure he recognized her, and told Harriet so. And she told Harriet Jack was probably sorry now about things he'd told Daphne while they were drinking together, those afternoons in Jamaica. Apparently, he really let his hair down with her."

"The odd couple," I suggested.

"The oddest," she agreed. "Jack was supposedly going to marry some actress, then, Stephanie something-or-other. His little blond Galatea with the big tits."

"She was in the movie in Jamaica, and that's why Jack was there."

"Right. The marriage never happened, of course. Jack was never a really plausible Pygmalion."

"Smart Stephanie," I suggested.

"Smart or lucky. From what Jack told Daphne back then, he was doing a real Charles Ward at that time."

"*The Lost Weekend*," I suggested.

I must have gotten it right, because she kept on going, saying, "He told Daphne there were other car accidents the police never caught him on, hit-and-run things, maybe even people who got killed."

"Lovely."

"*And* he was over his head financially. He told Daphne about some scheme he had for getting development money for movies that were never going to happen. I mean, out-and-out fraud. There was one British production company he hit pretty hard."

"And he *told* all this to Daphne?"

"Who of course told it to Harriet, who never passed any of it on to anybody before today. Except once, when a friend of hers in the business was thinking of hiring Jack for something, and Harriet advised against. So it looks," Bly said, "as though the moral of the story is, if you're going to commit fraud and manslaughter, don't drink, and if you're going to drink, don't— "

"Got it," I said. "So that's why Harriet thinks Jack is the one who killed Daphne."

"Sure. Harriet's convinced that Jack *did* recognize Daphne, and that's why he was so nervous and bad-tempered and Achilles right from the very beginning."

"But didn't he have to know Daphne would be here?" I asked. "He knew Harriet was coming, certainly, I mean he had to know who the cast was that he'd be directing in this spot—"

"Well, that's where his being a former drunk comes in," Bly said. "Harriet's theory is, since that week in the bar in Jamaica was three years ago, and Jack's gone off the sauce since then and was probably pretty blurry most of the time before he dried out, he probably *didn't* make the connection immediately when he took on this job. You realize, by the way, this public service work was another part of his sentence after the vehicular endangerment conviction."

"The same judge who sent him to AA?"

"That's right. Sentenced him to so many hours of public service work. So this would have counted toward that, which is what he would have been thinking about, and not some drunken dyke he told all his troubles to three years ago in Jamaica. Then, when he saw her at that airport and realized what a threat she was to him and his new safe and sane and sober life—"

"No," I said, shaking my head. "It doesn't scan. I don't see Jack moving like that at all. He might have confronted her, tried to bluster his way through. He might even have thrown himself on her mercy. But the most likely thing, I think, is that he'd try to pretend it didn't exist, bury his head in the sand and hope Daphne and the whole problem would go away."

"The hit-and-run personality, in other words."

"Sure. And the reason he was mad at Clement playing Sherlock Holmes with Daphne's death was that he saw how easily it could open up this whole can of worms about his own past life, when he's just in the process of burying it for good and all."

"One way and another," Bly said dryly.

"I just don't see it," I said. "I just don't see Jack cold-bloodedly killing Daphne like that, in such an elaborate way, and only to stop her just in case it turned out she felt like telling on him. And, for God's sake, Bly, even if she did start to tell stories out of school, it'd just be her word against his, and Jack French would still carry more clout in the world than Daphne Wheeler. And finally, why on earth would she? What's in it for Daphne to make trouble for Jack French?"

"All of these arguments have been presented to Harriet," Bly said, "by both Betsy and me, and she rejects them, every one. There is no question in her mind Jack French saw Daphne, recognized her, realized she was a threat—on the fraud business, more than old hit and runs that would be hard to prove now—and decided to take action right away. Harriet's reading of Jack is, the pressures of not drinking, plus the clear agony the man went through in that little plane coming out here, and then to see our pilot die right in front of us, drove Jack over the edge, and he did what he did. Then, when Clement was so brilliant and disproved the staged suicide, Jack panicked and hid somewhere. Either that, or he got out of the house, possibly dying himself in the process."

"Got out of the house *how*?"

Bly gestured at the windows, with the gray storm streaming outside. "Those windows open, you know."

"There's a sheer drop outside."

"Rope ladders? Sheets tied together?"

"In this wind? Besides, that would have left traces, like an open window, or a rope tied to a bed leg. As a matter of fact," I said, looking at the windows, "a murdered Jack might have been *thrown* out."

"That is another idea we considered," Bly told me. "Also, Harriet says, what if Jack became suicidal after his Daphne murder scheme didn't work, and threw *himself* out?"

"Oh, enough," I said, waving my hands in defeat, like Joseph Cotten in *The Third Man*. "There's too many possibilities, nothing concrete to work from. Leave it to Clement, let him play Sherlock Holmes with all this."

"As a matter of fact," Bly said, "that's the other

thing I have to tell you, why Clement is so keen to be the actual real-life brilliant detective in the case.''

"There's a reason? I thought it just came with the territory; he's been playing Sherlock so long, he's like that old story about the guy wearing the mask, and when he takes if off, his face has changed to look like the mask.''

"So the mob recognizes him, and tears him limb from limb.'' Bly nodded, frowning out at the storm. "I know that story too. Which one *is* that?''

"Bly,'' I said. "We were talking about Clement.''

"Oh, right. Well, you know about this new TV series he's got coming up.''

"He's delighted about it.''

"He's terrified of it,'' Bly corrected me. "Betsy told me the whole thing.''

"What do you mean? He doesn't want to do it?''

"He loves the idea,'' Bly said, "but the network's scheduled it at eight o'clock.''

"The kid time.''

"Exactly. And he's been put up against a long-run popular show, something to do with rock music. The network Clement's with, they've tried going into that time slot with other obvious kid-oriented stuff, but they get slaughtered every time, so the idea is to go in with something absolutely different and try for some *other* audience.''

"The smart kids.''

"The whoever,'' Bly said. "Puzzle fans, detective fans, they don't care. Just so it's enough to build a Neilsen. But it's a gamble. It's such a gamble, the network has ordered only six episodes.''

"So they don't have a lot of confidence.''

"Not a whole lot. In fact, at first they ordered only *three* episodes, but the producer got them up to six on the basis that ordering three was declaring it a failure in advance."

"Which it is, of course."

"Which it is, of course," Bly agreed. "If you order only three, and the thing hits, there isn't time to order more, and there goes the time slot. Even with six, it's scary; you have to hit right away, there isn't time to build. Which is why Clement sees this whole situation as a publicity bonanza, much to Betsy's embarrassment."

"Oh, I see," I said. "Just in time for the new Sherlock Holmes series on TV, here's Clement Hasbrouck solving the baffling murders of Munro's Island."

Bly nodded. "Betsy quite rightly sees this as being in rather bad taste. But she says Clement insists they'd be stupid not to take advantage of a situation dumped in their laps like this."

"So he's in competition with Fred and Harriet and me, of course," I said. "Whether we are with him or not. Which explains the odd feeling I've been getting from him. And also explains why he's been going so nuts over what happened to Jack French."

"He hasn't been able to solve it. Bad for publicity."

"He was actually calling Jack's name down in the refinery," I said, "as though he were a lost puppy or something."

"Come back, little Jack," Bly said, suddenly getting lithely up from the bed.

"Hey, wait a minute," I said, reaching for her, but too late. "Come back, little Bly. What's going on?"

"I have to wash my hair." she said, moving off toward the bathroom. "There's something about searching a castle that makes one grimy.'' Laughing at the expression on my face, she said, ''Don't worry, I'll be back.''

''All wet.''

''You can dry me,'' she promised, and went away to the bathroom.

But she was back sooner than either of us had anticipated, looking discontented, saying, ''Drat.''

''What's wrong?''

''The water's barely lukewarm.''

''Well, so were you.''

''Now, don't be mean,'' she said. ''I just wanted to be my cleanest for you.''

''Come here, Bly,'' I said. ''While the water's getting hot, why don't you and me do the same.''

19

"**S**am."

I woke up, instantly, and saw Bly leaning over me, wearing her robe and her grin. "Num," I said, to demonstrate that I was perfectly wide awake and capable of all necessary responses.

"It's Clement," she said.

Almost all necessary responses. I frowned at her through sudden clouds. "*What's* Clement?"

"At the door. He wants to know if you can come out and play."

When had I fallen asleep? Sometime after the water had become hot again, which was sometime after Bly had discovered it wasn't hot. So what time was it now? I asked Bly, who said, "Ten minutes to six."

Beyond the windows was a kind of roiling darkness in lieu of a sunset. I said, "And Clement wants . . ."

"Your aid and support, is how he phrased it."

"Tell him to give me two minutes," I said, throwing off the covers and getting out of bed.

129

In fact, it took six minutes, and then I found Clement down one level in the guest parlor, where he'd told Bly he would wait for me. With him was Fred, looking as bemused as I felt. "Hello, Clement," I said. "I'm afraid I dropped off for a while."

"We all did," Fred told me with satisfaction.

"We all needed our rest," Clement announced with the faintest hint of disapproval. "But it has now occurred to me that there's one more potentially useful move we might make."

Fred and I glanced at each other. Fred said, "What's that, Clement?"

"Search Jack's room," he said.

Astonished, I said, "Jack isn't in his *room*, Clement!"

"Not looking for Jack, certainly not," he said. "But he will have left all his personal possessions and clothing behind. It seemed to me there might be some indication, some suggestion of what had happened, some, umm . . ."

"Clue?" I asked.

"In a word, yes," he agreed, unabashed. "Something that might cast more light on this situation. I see nothing to be lost by the attempt, do you?"

"Except time," said Fred.

"We have plenty of that, I think," Clement said dryly. "In any event, I didn't want to take the responsibility on myself of going into his room alone for the search. If you two are willing, I'd prefer you to accompany me."

Well, well. Even Sherlock never had this; two Watsons at once. Still, there just might be sense in Clement's idea after all, so I said, "Be happy to accompany you."

"Me, too," said Fred, though grinning.

Clement ignored the grin. "Come along, then," he said, turning away.

Fred beamed at me, having a whole lot of fun. "Come, Holt," he said sternly. "The game's afoot."

We went through the Hasbroucks' bedroom, where we found Betsy reading in a chair by the stormy windows. She gave us a mild look as we trooped through, and Clement told her, "We're just having a look at Jack's room, my dear."

"Of course," she said without much interest, and went back to her reading.

As we went through the shared bathroom, I saw that Clement or Betsy had rearranged Jack's toiletries from their former spread-out mess to a neat cluster at the end of the counter farthest from their own sink. It included a number of patent and prescription medicines for stomach troubles and headaches, both liquids and pills.

Jack's room itself was somewhat messy, but it was a normal kind of mess, not the sort that might have been caused by a struggle. His clothing hung in the closet—I noticed he had more clothes along for this short stay than George had, who was more or less living here—and filled two dresser drawers. There were no notes or letters, nothing written that had any bearing on Jack's disappearance.

On the bedside table was a copy of the cancer spot script, covered all over with crabbed writing in green ink; Jack's notes to himself about the shoot. They were hard to read, but I persevered, and every one of them was about the job at hand—suggestions about camera angles, methods of entrance, moves the actors might make, things like that. I hadn't actually seen the script before, so, while Fred and Clement continued to open drawers and look under the bed, I skimmed quickly through it, and found it even worse than I'd expected, more foolish and banal and embarrassing. If this shoot ever did take place, there'd be some changes made. Though the whole job was looking more and more doubtful.

I had come down here to be involved in something I already knew was absurd, that I didn't really want to be part of, and now it had turned into something else and worse. Absurdity with claws. I didn't myself know exactly what I meant, I knew only that real murder, real tragedy, and a real disappearance had been turned into something stupid and farcical, something I would want to dissociate myself from even more firmly than from this cancer script as presently written. But I was stuck in this burlesque, helpless, unable to walk away from it or alter it in any way. It wasn't possible to rewrite Daphne Wheeler's death or Jack French's disappearance.

"Nothing," Fred said. "Nice try, Clement, but there's nothing here."

Clement looked around, unsatisfied. "I thought surely . . ." His voice trailed off.

Fred said, "Well, at least we have one dog that didn't bark in the night."

"That's not particularly amusing," Clement told him, while I, still with the script in my hand, looked over and said, "Which dog is that?"

"The booze hound. There's no liquor or empty bottles hidden in here."

"So the idea that he fell off the wagon . . ."

"Remains unproved," Fred said.

"Well, that's something," I agreed, and turned back

to drop the script on the bedside table. The bed was made, but loosely, the covers just having been thrown over it when Jack got up this morning. "Maybe there's something under the pillow," I suggested, and lifted the pillow, and there was nothing.

"Maybe he's hiding in the bed," Fred suggested.

"Let's see." I grabbed the top sheet and blanket, flipped them back, and looked down at the initials D and W in shaky letters a foot long. They had been made by pouring some liquid in long lines onto the bottom sheet. The liquid had dried to a kind of dusky rose color, with many cracks, like land in a drought, or like a scab.

"Good God!" Clement said, coming over to stare past my arm. "Daphne Wheeler!"

"Looks that way," I said.

Wide-eyed, Clement half-whispered, "Is it blood?"

Fred had also come over to the bed. Licking a finger, he touched the top to the bottom corner of the D, then tasted it. We watched him, and his expression became utterly bewildered, almost frightened.

"Well?" Clement demanded. "Is it blood?"

"No." Fred shook his head, frowning in what I now saw was irritation. "Is this supposed to be funny?"

"Well, what is it?" I asked him.

He looked at me. "Pepto-Bismol," he said.

20

I think it was mostly bewilderment that made us decide not to tell the others about this latest discovery. Who had written those letters, and why? If it was meant to be a message to the rest of us, it was a strangely obscure place to leave it. There had been a very good chance, in fact, that nobody would find this message or whatever it was until the bed linen was changed, which would probably be by George and certainly not till after this entire episode was over and we'd all made our way back to the mainland.

But if it wasn't a message, what in hell *was* it? The initials had to refer to Daphne Wheeler, but to what end? Fred started to float the idea that it was meant as some sort of memorium, put there by Harriet, who was one of those who believed Jack French to be guilty of Daphne's murder, but even while he was explaining the idea, he was already shaking his head, disagreeing with himself. "Never mind, never mind," he said. "Even if Harriet was weird enough to scrawl Daphne's initials

134

around in honor of her blessed memory, she wouldn't leave them in Jack's *bed*."

"Psychologically quite unlikely," Clement agreed.

"The whole goddamn thing is unlikely," I said. I was feeling irritable, as though somebody were pulling my leg, as though I were in the middle of some dumb practical joke. But Daphne Wheeler was dead, that was no joke. Jack French was presumably dead, his body probably thrown out a window to be disposed of by the storm, and that was no joke. Was the broken radio a joke? If these dribbled initials were not a joke, what were they?

"Perhaps," Clement said uncertainly, "it's a message of revenge."

Fred said, "How's that? Revenge for what?"

"I don't have much confidence in this myself," Clement admitted, "but what if the message is supposed to be that Jack French was killed to avenge the death of Daphne Wheeler?"

I said, "*Two* murderers? Jack killed Daphne, for whatever reason, and then somebody else—and I suppose you mean Harriet—killed Jack?"

"It doesn't seem to make sense, does it?" he said, frowning over his little idea as though it were a tiny fire in an Arctic camp; inadequate, but all he had.

I said, "The reason it doesn't make sense, besides the fact that there was no guarantee anybody was ever going to see this thing, is that Jack's body itself would be the best way to show a message of revenge. If the killer wants to say, 'I did this to avenge the death of Daphne Wheeler,' the way to do it is to leave the body around where it can be found, not hide it or dispose of it and then write initials in the bed."

"Yes," Clement said, nodding reluctantly. "That is the crux of the problem right there, the disappearing body. I just feel, if we could only find out what happened to Jack, we'd be much further along the way."

Fred shook his head at the initials on the sheet. "The damnedest thing," he said. "It's a message, and yet it isn't. It's meant to be found, I mean it has to have been put there in order to be found, and at the same time it might never have been found."

"If we hadn't chosen to search this room," Clement pointed out.

"If you hadn't thought of doing it," Fred told him. "And even so, we were ready to leave. We were almost going out the door when Sam pulled the covers back."

I said, "Because you made that joke about Jack hiding in the bed."

"That's right." Fred dropped into Charlie Chan, but looked at us both ironically as he singsonged, "Other man's brain like room without doors: may be full of riches, but impossible to gain entry."

I said, "In other words, one of us could be responsible, and knew how to make sure the message would be found."

Fred said, "Clement, was it your idea to search in here, or did somebody else suggest it?"

"Mine, I'm afraid," Clement said. "Which makes me the prime suspect, I suppose."

"Or me," I said. "I'm the one turned the covers down. Or Fred, with his little joke. But in fact, the idea that we might decide to look through Fred's things isn't so unlikely. If none of us had come up with it on our own, then whoever did this could have made the suggestion later on."

Fred said, "Who searched this part of the house the first time through?"

"My wife," Clement said, "with Mort Weinstein."

"I'd like to know," Fred said, "if *they* turned the covers down."

I said, "You mean, you think this might have been done afterward? Why?"

"Just flailing around," he told me with a shrug. "I'd like to know, that's all."

"I'll be happy to ask Betsy," Clement said. "Just a moment."

He left, going through the connecting bedroom, and I said to Fred, "There's something I forgot to ask you before. When we came back upstairs I was going to ask, but then the radio was broken and that knocked it out of my mind."

"Sure," he said. "What is it?"

"When we were down in the basements on the second search, Clement and Mort and me, the floor in front of one of the windows in the armory was wet, as though the window had been open for some time. But it was closed."

"I closed it," Fred said. "Crosby and I looked in there, and the window was half open, just enough to let in a lot of cold and a little rain. I don't know how long it had been like that. Since before the storm, probably, and what with everything else going on, Danny and Mort must have forgot all about it. So we closed it."

"Mort was surprised at the idea it had been open," I said.

"Oh, yeah? You think it means anything?"

I said, "By now, I don't know if *anything* means anything."

Clement came back, shaking his head, saying, "She isn't there. It's well after six, she's probably gone down to the observation room for drinks."

"Drinks," said Fred. "What a good idea."

"We can ask her when we go down there," I said.

"Which raises the question," Clement said, "of what we tell the others about *that*." And he made a long-fingered graceful gesture at the initials.

We looked at one another. I could see my own reluctance echoed in both their faces, but it took Fred to give us a justification for what we all obviously wanted to do anyway. "If we don't say anything," he told us, "then whoever did this might get the idea his message wasn't received, and it might make him do something else to attract our attention."

"Do we want that?" Clement asked him.

"Yes, we do," Fred said, nodding. "We want our weird killer friend out and about, making moves. That's the only way we're ever going to find him."

"Oh, he's out and about," I said. "He's making moves, Fred, that's not the problem. I'm pretty sure he isn't finished with us yet, and I don't much like his sense of humor, so we'd better find him as soon as we can. But you're right. If we don't mention this thing here"—and I covered the initials again, leaving the bed as it had been before—"it might throw him off balance a little, and that can only help."

21

Betsy Hasbrouck, according to Clement, didn't remember whether or not she and Mort had turned down the bedclothes in Jack French's room during the first search. "She's quite curious," he said with a crooked smile, having drawn me to one side of the observation room to give me this news; or lack of news. "You know how women get. But I have assured her it was merely an idle question on my part. Unfortunately, her answer is far from satisfactory."

"I'll ask Mort," I volunteered, "when I have a chance."

"Very good. Though what Fred might have in mind with this particular question, I cannot begin to guess."

I could, if only vaguely. "We'll give him his head, that's all," I said, leaving it to Clement to decide whether I meant Fred or the killer.

Then I returned to Bly and my drink, and she said, "What was that all about?"

"Tell you later," I said, because of course I would.

And Clement, whether he knew it or not, would also be explaining the situation to Betsy. I wondered how close, in something like this, Fred and Crosby were.

We were all in the observation room now, at about half past six, except Danny and George, who were in the kitchen working on dinner. Clement and Betsy and Harriet—Harriet looking somewhat recovered, but still grim—were one conversational cluster, on a pair of right-angled sofas by the rear wall, where they could ignore the angry twilight beyond the windows. Fred and Crosby, with many comic remarks at each other, were playing backgammon in another part of the room, seated on chairs facing each other over a table containing a backgammon board. And Mort was at the bar, making himself a drink.

Outside, the storm seemed neither larger nor smaller than before, but simply a fact, as though we were on some other and more violent planet, far from Earth, where this was the normal weather. With the radio out, we had no idea of the forecast, of how much longer we could expect to be isolated here.

Knocking back my Jack Daniel's and water, I took Bly's not quite empty glass and said, "I'll make refills."

"I'll watch the tournament," she decided, and headed over to kibitz Fred and Crosby while I joined Mort at the bar.

He gave me a rueful grin, saying, "Some fun, eh? Too bad PACKARD's off the air. You could use this as one of the stories."

"It would need a hell of a rewrite," I told him.

He chuckled his agreement and said, "Well, it can't last much longer."

"Let's hope not. Mort, let me ask a dumb question."

"Of course."

"When you and Betsy went through Jack French's room, was there anything *odd* in there? Anything that struck you as, I don't know, not normal in any way?"

He considered that, watching me make drinks for Bly and myself. "Hints, you mean," he said. "Anything that might suggest what happened to Jack."

"Right. Of course, I realize you were just looking for Jack himself, so you wouldn't have been opening drawers and all that—"

"As a matter of fact, we did," Mort said. "Betsy's very fierce when she's on her own, you know. That nervous eager little bird she does is just when she's around Clement."

I nodded, saying, "I'd already figured that out."

"The first thing she said when we went into Jack's room was, 'Let's see if he left a note.' So we looked everywhere in the room that a note might have been left. Including in all the drawers."

"And under the pillow?" I asked, grinning as though it was supposed to be a joke.

"Sure, under the pillow. And under the bed. We were looking for bottles, too, you know, and, by the way, we didn't find any."

"Under the pillow, inside the bed . . . I guess you pulled the covers back too."

"We must have." Then he shrugged, saying, "If you want, why not toss the place yourself? Maybe you'll see some—"

"We already did," I told him. "Clement and Fred and me. We didn't find a thing."

He gave me a keen look. "So you wanted to know if anything had been changed, anything taken away."

"Something like that."

"Well, there was nothing out of the ordinary when Betsy and I went through, and that's for sure. And it was the same when you were up there, right?"

"So that's that," I said, avoiding the lie direct. Then I carried the fresh drinks back over to Bly and we sat in a corner of the observation room, well away from everybody else, while I told her the whole story.

There's an expression Bly gets in her eye every once in a while that I think of as her plot-maven look. Being a writer of television sitcoms, she lives with those simple threads of storyline on which one strings the broad dialogue that goes in front of the laughtrack. It's impossible work unless you have a knack for it, like Bly, in which case it's apparently very easy. And from time to time I can see her busy brain reducing the circumstances of reality to the dimensions of a sitcom plot, looking for the storyline, the useful pegs, the broadly laid-in motivations. She had that look in her eye when I finished telling her about the initials in Jack French's bed, and I said to her, "There's no laughtrack on this one, Bly."

"Somebody," she said darkly, "is playing a double game."

"Of course. The question is, who?"

Here's where her strength lay, in the sorting out of the characters. "It was Fred who asked the question," she said, "whether or not the initials had been there during the first search. But why did he ask it?"

"I don't know."

"It's a strange question to ask. Particularly when it turns out he's right, the initials *were* added later."

"Betsy doesn't remember if they turned the bed down

or not, and Mort just said, 'We must have.' So there's still some slight doubt.''

"Very slight doubt," she insisted. "I just wish I knew why Fred thought it was a question worth asking in the first place.''

"I can't help you," I told her, "and my impression is, he wouldn't tell me his reasons if I asked. But somehow I have the feeling it has something to do with Jack not being found, the idea that the lack of a body forced somebody to do something else, make some further gesture.''

"The murderer, or somebody else?''

"Beats me.''

"Well, all right," she said, giving it up, "so that's Fred. Then there's Clement. Why did he come up with this idea to search Jack's room in the first place?''

"I have two thoughts on that one," I said. "To begin with, Clement's the one who feels the need to be investigating this thing, finding clues, solving the murder for publicity reasons.''

"Creepy enough already," Bly commented.

"Granted. Beyond that, Clement's the sort of guy who'd have no trouble absorbing somebody else's idea and making it his own. Anybody else at all could have mentioned casually in his presence that it might be a good idea to take a look through Jack's room, and half an hour later Clement would be honestly convinced it was his own stroke of inspiration.''

Bly looked past me at the rest of the room. "So it could be any one of them.''

"Maybe even any two of them," I said. "Mort and Danny, for instance, are partners. If the motive's something to do with money or business, it could involve them both and they could both be behind what's going on here. And they certainly know the territory better than the rest of us.''

"You mean, invite a bunch of people to your isolated house and then bump them off one by one? I've seen that movie.''

A full-throated laugh from Crosby, over at the backgammon table, made me say, "All right, then, what about Fred and Crosby? Can you see them working together as a team?''

"To commit murder? Not a chance." But then she frowned at them across the room, considering the idea, and finally she said, "But you can't ever be absolutely sure about anybody, can you?''

"Fred said that himself, up in Jack's room. Some Charlie Chan thing about the human brain being a room without doors or some such thing.''

"What we don't know," Bly said, "and this is the big problem, we don't know *motive*. Who among us would have a strong reason to kill Daphne *and* a strong reason to kill Jack?''

"An unlikely pairing," I agreed. "So far as anybody knows, the only link between them is that one week in Jamaica three years ago. And the only other people tied to that week are George and Harriet.''

"I don't see either of them—" Bly started to say, but then she broke off and shook her head. "I don't see anybody," she confessed. "That's the scary part of it. Because it can't be anybody, it could be everybody. Ten very different people.''

"Not you, and not me," I pointed out.

"Which leaves eight." Bly looked across the room again. "And then there were eight." She shook her head. "I wonder what's going to happen next," she said.

22

It didn't happen until after a dinner that had started very quiet and gloomy, but which, mostly through the help of a good supply of wine and the determination of Fred and Crosby to keep the tiny flame of light conversation alive, gradually became convivial, almost normal. Harriet unbent a bit, but every time she started to relax and take part in the conversation, you could see memory yank hard on the reins, pulling her head up, giving a hard bright shine to her eyes.

Fred raised the subject of the western, the one-time hardy perennial of both movies and television, presenting as his topic: Whatever-happened-to-it? "There was a time," he reminded us, "when probably a quarter of the product coming out of Hollywood was some kind of western. My father played a chuck-wagon cook so many times, he was given an honorary degree by some culinary institute, and at home he couldn't fry water."

I said, "Your father was an actor? I didn't know that."

"Oh, sure," Fred said, grinning. "I am a pure product of nepotism, got my first part playing my father's son in a *Good Earth* ripoff for Republic Pictures. I was four. My father didn't think the name Li sounded Oriental enough, it was too much like that Civil War general, so his professional name was Malcolm Wu."

"I remember that name," I said, and a couple of other people at the table said they remembered it too.

"His big years were during the Second World War," Fred told us. "Evil Japanese interrogators. You round-eyes can never tell Japanese from Chinese anyway, so he did fine." Dropping into nasality, with a clipped accent, very unlike his Charlie Chan, he said, "I were edoocated in your country. UCRA."

"Yeah, I'm a little guy," Bly snarled at him, "but there's a million more little guys just like me. And they're on their way, Hirohito."

Still clipped and nasal, Fred told her, "They will not help *you*, G.I." Then, reverting to his own voice, he said, "But never mind my father. The question is westerns. What happened to them? Why can't *I* play a chuck-wagon cook? They were all over the lot—" Groucho imitation: "And I do mean the studio lot." Own voice again: "—then all at once they dried up. Producers try to make one every once in a while now, but nobody goes to see them. Even Clint Eastwood can't sell tickets anymore, not if he's on a horse, and on television they're gone, gone, gone."

"I think," Clement said, "they were plagued by a certain sameness. The audience simply grew tired of them."

"With all respect, Clement," Fred said, though I

myself very much doubted the respect, "what you and I do is not usually brimful of originality."

"Besides," Crosby said, "they'd already been un-original for years, and everybody still liked them. The twenty-fifth Jimmy Stewart western, he was even still wearing that same sheepskin coat, but people went to see it. The hundredth episode of *Gunsmoke* wasn't going to be *that* different from the first, but people watched it."

"Something happened in the society," Harriet said. This was one of her rare entries into the conversation, and everybody looked at her with a certain cautious hope as she said, "Certain values exemplified by the western became less regarded, that's all. The grandiose science fiction films represent the new values."

Bly said, "Which values?"

Harriet said, "Society at the moment values technology and team spirit, group effort, as in all those *Star Wars* films. The western glorified the individual man, dependent on his own skills and talents. For the comic element, the western favored innocent sexual awkwardness, and the new films favor corrupt sexual awkwardness."

I watched Fred blink at Harriet, trying to figure out what to say next, now that his light conversational gambit had suddenly veered into these murky waters. But before he could find a way back to the shallows, Danny suddenly said with an undertone of anger, "That's a part of it, Harriet, but the truth is actually simpler than that. The western killed itself."

Fred looked at him warily. "How?"

"By deconstruction," Danny told him. "A literary technique that perhaps works in French, but when I see it in a script in English, I tend to throw the script against the wall.''

"Hold on there," Bly said, "Deconstruction has its place.''

"In the wastebasket," Danny said firmly.

"I'm not so sure about that," Bly told him, and I knew what was bothering her. In her early career, before she'd moved out to Hollywood to join the sitcom sausage factory, she'd had a number of short stories published in the slick magazines, that were then collected into a book titled *Hesitation Cuts*. The ideas and techniques of the deconstructionists had influenced several of those stories, and that's why Bly now said, "Deconstruction can be very valuable. Why isn't heightened awareness a good thing?''

"Wait a second," Crosby said, holding her hand up like a traffic cop. "You all lost me on that last turn. What in holy hell is deconstruction?''

With a polite gesture toward Bly, Danny said, "I think its defender should have the right to describe it.''

"Sure," Bly said, and told Crosby, "The idea is to be *aware* that the story is a story. The way Brecht in the theater always used distancing techniques to prevent the audience from becoming too caught up in the play. He didn't want people to forget they were watching a play, and that the play had a meaning they should be thinking about, to agree with or disagree with.''

Harriet said, "The play is an argument.''

"That's right," Bly said. "The deconstructionists do the same thing. You're going to tell a story, fine. The story is in a genre, maybe a western or a mystery or a war story or whatever you want. In each genre there are basic patterns, recurring scenes, stock characters. So with the deconstructionists the story is aware that it's a story, the characters are aware that they're characters with a function to fulfill, and the reader or the audience is constantly being reminded that this isn't real life, this is a pattern, and it's being presented in a particular way because of various artistic decisions and to further some sort of argument. The deconstructionist doesn't try to sneak up on the audience and slip the propaganda in without anybody noticing.''

Crosby said, ''What do you mean, the story's aware it's a story?''

''By referring to itself,'' Bly told her, ''and by referring to the whole line of stories that came before it in that genre. In a western, the tough but honest foreman is aware that he's an archetype, that Ward Bond is the basic figure he's modeled after, and that the purpose he's been created for is to represent that element of the story and not to live a regular life like a regular human being. He *knows* he's a Kabuki mask, and once we all agree that's what he is, then he can comment on and even disagree with the values his character represents. Like Harvey Korman in *Blazing Saddles,* who *knew* he was playing the smooth evil saloon owner and was delighted at how well he was doing the part.''

''That's the trouble with deconstruction right there,'' Danny said. ''You can't tell a straight serious story with it. You can only do comedy, and the comedy usually comes out pretty goddamn arch. Once you've got westerns like *Dirty Dingus Magee* and *Goin' South,* where the actors spend all their time winking at the audience, the western was through. Audiences thought they were being made fun of, and audiences don't like that. So they left the wise guys winking and grinning and making believe they were hip, and the audience went somewhere else."

"Including, one hopes," Clement said, "back to Sherlock Holmes."

"Hear, hear," I said, because I thought it would please Clement, and it did, and Mort said, "Not to change the subject, but I remember I worked with Malcolm Wu once, years ago, when I was just barely in the business, and I always wondered where he got that English accent."

"From Basil Rathbone," Fred told him, and that changed the subject, and we continued in a lighter vein for the rest of the meal, though Harriet made no further effort to join in. Looking over at her, seeing her poke abstractedly at her food, I was sorry we hadn't had more conversation together before Daphne Wheeler's death had closed her down. I suspected there was a good brain behind that imperious manner and fusty Miss Marple exterior. I remembered, when we'd first met at the airport in Nicaragua, and Bly had asked if there had ever been a president before Nixon whose name started with N, Harriet had immediately answered no. Most of us would have spent a few seconds, at least, trying to remember the thirty-some names involved.

Announcing that this was the last of the fresh fruit, Danny and George finished the meal with plates of mango and melon, to have with our coffee. Everyone had coffee, since clearly no one was in a hurry to go to bed and to sleep tonight.

It was a strange meal in many ways. We were in a tense and difficult and weirdly unusual situation, but periods of normalcy just kept breaking through. People are primarily themselves, no matter what the deconstructionists say, and are only secondarily players in whatever drama they may find themselves in.

There was an unspoken desire among us all to stick together, not to go off into solitary corners, so after dinner we all went back to the observation room, which at night had become a kind of stage set of itself, reflected back from the black windows concealing the storm. We could watch ourselves move here and there around a room which was shaped more like a stage than a normal room anyway, being so wide and shallow. There were two of each of us, the real one and the one in the glass, the observer and the observed. It forced a kind of artificiality on us, a self-consciousness in our movements, a brittleness in our voices.

Danny and George joined the rest of us shortly after dinner, Danny spending a while showing Clement our location on various Caribbean maps while George fiddled fretfully with the broken radio, in the forlorn hope that he could bring it back to life and get in touch again with his Blondel. Betsy and Harriet read books in companionable silence together. Bly and I began by kibitzing the backgammon tourney, which had picked up again immediately after dinner, but soon we joined in, working out a complicated rotation scheme with Fred and Crosby where the winner got to retain his seat and play the next game. Fred was either very good or very lucky—very good, I suspect—and rarely lost, so it became simply the three of us against him in doomed round-robin succession. And Mort, playing the good host in these extremely strange conditions, kept moving around, circulating among us, entering into brief conversations here and there, offering after-dinner drinks or more coffee.

The groups shifted from time to time, Bly joining Clement and Danny and the maps at one point when Fred had bounced her from the backgammon board yet again, and Crosby under similar circumstances going over to see how George was doing with the radio. I was Fred's opponent at that time, living in a sea of blots, glancing around from time to time as Fred with his wicked grin shook the dice cup and rolled his double sixes. Seeing Crosby and George together, bending over the strewn remains of the radio, it occurred to me just how many possible different pairings and groupings there were among these ten people. Those were the only two blacks, over there, in direct conversation for the first time that I was aware of. How many other links were there among us, real or fancied, obvious or obscure?

Harriet, Fred, Clement, and I shared a commonality, however reluctant I might be to admit it. Danny, who I vaguely remembered had entered show business as a chorus line dancer before becoming a producer, shared with Crosby that kind of experience of musical theater. Harriet and Clement shared a background in legitimate theater that none of the rest of us possessed. Was Harriet the only homosexual, or did she share that with Danny, about whom I couldn't make up my mind? Was Mort the only Jew? Betsy was the only wife, and Clement the only husband. Fred the only Oriental. Bly and I the only writers. And Betsy in a way was the only civilian, the only one of us with no direct personal relationship with show business, one way or another.

The groups kept shifting. I lost again, and Crosby took my place, and I went over to look at maps with Danny and Bly, Clement having moved on to a conversation with Harriet and Betsy and Mort. (Betsy seemed perfectly contented to have her reading interrupted, but I noticed that Harriet was marking her place with her finger in the closed book. Her natural imperiousness was recovering itself.)

"We are really way to hell and gone," Bly said, as I walked up. "I begin to feel like Gilligan."

"Clement was asking me," Danny explained, "if there was any island nearby that a boat could reach us from, before planes are able to land here, and the answer is no, there really isn't. As Bly says, we are to hell and gone."

His fingertip tapped the map. I leaned close and saw the tiny black ragged dot surrounded by blue and identified in small black letters as Munro's Island. A few other tiny islands were some distance away to the east, but the nearest land mass of any size had to be at least two hundred miles from here. "I see," I said.

"We're on the highest peak of a mountain range," Danny said. "The rest of the mountaintops don't break the surface of the water."

"Sonny Trager's Shangri-La." I looked around, seeing myself in the windows, looking around. "I'm coming to the conclusion," I said, "that Sonny Trager had a misspent youth in front of the television set. He loved those old movies so much he decided to live in them."

"Coke dreams," Danny said with a faint grimace of contempt. "They all want to live in their fantasies. That's what sends them to the drug in the first place."

"When you wish upon a star," Bly said.

I said, "Was Sonny Trager a user too?"

"Of course," Danny said with another show of contempt. "You don't get into that business unless you're bent that way already. I've known only one dealer who wasn't a junkie himself, and that was a special case.''

''Who was that?'' Bly asked.

But Danny grinned at her, shaking his head. ''That would be telling.''

Crosby called to Bly that it was her turn to batter herself against the impregnable Fred. She went away, and I said to Danny, ''What about what's going on here? Does this all look like the work of a junkie to you?''

He looked startled by the idea. ''Good God, do you think so?''

''I have no idea. I'm grabbing at straws. The damn thing has to make sense from *some* direction, but I just haven't found it yet.''

''It would explain a number of things,'' he said thoughtfully.

''Except where the junk is coming from.''

He frowned, not seeing the problem. ''Wouldn't he have brought it with him?''

I gestured at the people around us, and in the windows my other self gestured at the other people around him. ''Which of these people would take a chance on carrying drugs on a commercial international flight? I don't know about anybody else, but Bly and I were shaken down pretty well both at LAX and in New Orleans.''

''It's been done,'' Danny said.

''People get caught.''

He grinned and shook his head, saying, ''That's how we know it's being done. We don't know what percentage of people get caught.''

''If you have a famous name, Danny,'' I said, ''let

me promise you, they give you a lot of attention at airports. They *love* to nab a celeb.''

''Unfortunately true.'' Danny shrugged. ''Dangerous for associates of ours sometimes. But look at these people.'' And now it was he and his mirror self who gestured at the rest of both casts as he said, ''Do you see any junkies here?''

''Not all dopers are that obvious.''

''Granted. But I just can't—'' He shook his head, looking from person to person. ''I don't see it. Frankly, all we had here was a couple of drunks, and they're both dead.'' Then his eyes widened, and he looked at me, saying, ''By God, that's right, isn't it? Both drunks, and both dead.''

That was a grouping that hadn't occurred to me. ''I can't think what that would mean,'' I said.

''Is our killer out to rid the world of alcoholics?'' With a grin, Danny said, ''He's set himself a task, in that case.''

''That's not going to get us anywhere,'' I said, and across the room Betsy Hasbrouck toppled forward out of her chair toward her toppling mirror image and thudded without a word onto the floor.

23

Clement had left Betsy and Harriet just before that, and the women had gone back to their reading while Clement had wandered over to watch George poke and pry at the radio, which he was now treating like some old jigsaw puzzle found in an attic and probably missing pieces. Mort and Crosby had been kibitzing the backgammon game between Fred and Bly, which had apparently been going Bly's way for a change, to everybody's astonishment. And Danny and I were talking together over the open map. We were all of us absorbed in what we were doing or saying, and yet every one of us saw Betsy fall.

I suppose we'd been waiting for it, subconsciously alert to it, like a herd of impala who know there's a lion somewhere about. The events on this island weren't finished yet, the killer wasn't done with us yet, and we all understood that. A part of each of us waited, tense, for whatever would happen next. And so, when the *event* occurred, we all immediately reacted, every eye in the room turning to Betsy before she'd even finished falling, and long before Clement's scream.

In fact, the only astonishing thing was that it was *Betsy*. I'd had no real opinion about where the next blow would fall, but somehow I'd never thought the ones of us at risk included Betsy. I'd expected someone more active and forceful.

Now that I thought about it, another element common to both Daphne and Jack, which Danny hadn't mentioned, was that both had been bad-tempered, and both had made public scenes before they were killed—if Jack had been killed. But Betsy was the reverse of that, civilized, helpful, obsequious to her husband, and with everybody else strong in a good way.

Then who should it have been instead? None of the rest of us had made bad public displays, and the only one of us who seemed to me generally bad-tempered was Danny; contempt and irritation and impatience kept leaching through all his polite conversations, as though from some limitless black lake of misanthropy within.

But it was Betsy who fell, and then Clement screamed with a chilling high-pitched sound, and the rest of us ran to where she lay crumpled on the floor, Harriet recoiling in her chair, pulling back, staring in horror as though she'd just learned Betsy had leprosy. Mort and I both went to our knees beside Betsy, but Crosby pushed at our shoulders, saying, "Let me in there, let me in there, I know about this."

We stood and moved aside, letting her through. Frowning at her, I said, "You *know* about this?"

"I'm a nurse," Crosby said astonishingly, while with one hand she smoothed down Betsy's rucked-up skirt and with her other reached for Betsy's left wrist.

Mort said, "A *nurse*?"

Behind us, Bly and Fred and Danny were trying to control Clement, who kept on wailing and keening and demanding something be done. "Blame my mama," Crosby said, then matter-of-factly added, "We have a pulse."

Harriet, her initial instinctive terror gone, had now leaned forward in her chair, propelled by curiosity. Unbelieving, she said, "She's alive?"

"And breath," Crosby reported, her hand now over Betsy's nose and mouth. "Pulse fast and light, breathing heavy and slow."

"Pick her up!" Clement cried. "Don't leave her on the floor!"

"No," Crosby said. "Not till we find out what the problem is."

Slowly she turned Betsy onto her back, with a pillow from a nearby chair to go under her head. She straightened the older woman's legs, arranged her arms at her sides, and bent low to listen to her heartbeat, then gently lifted each of Betsy's eyelids, studying the blank, glistening eyes. Meantime, Fred was explaining, "Crosby's mama is a very strong lady, and she never did believe much in showbiz."

"Still doesn't," Crosby said, and bent again to sniff at Betsy's nose and mouth.

"So they made a deal," Fred went on. "Mama would help while Crosby tried to become a singer, but only if Crosby went to nursing school, so she'd have something to fall back on when the showbiz career fizzled out."

"Mama's an R.N.," Crosby said, studying Betsy's arms and legs and the sides of her neck. "It's what she understands and believes in."

"I've met Mama," Fred went on, "and if she told *me* to go to nursing school, I'd go."

"Clement," Crosby called over her shoulder, "what medication does Betsy take?"

Bly and Danny permitted Clement forward now, but kept their hands on him. Wild-eyed, his longish hair in damp raggy ribbons on his forehead and neck, he said, "Is she truly alive? Truly?"

"At the moment," Crosby said, brisk and impersonal and deliberately harsh. "Tell me what medication she takes."

The tone startled Clement into cooperation. "Oh, well, not any— Not really, only her muscle relaxant, that's the only—"

"What is it?" Crosby demanded. "What's it called?"

"I don't really know," Clement told her. He was washing his hands together, bending forward like a supplicant. "Do you think it mixes with the other? Is that possible?"

"I won't know until I know what it is," Crosby told him.

"Well, it's a— She has these muscle spasms sometimes, in her neck and back, the doctor gave her—"

"Pills?"

"Yes."

"Where are they?"

"They should be—" He looked vaguely about for a couple of seconds, then spotted his wife's bag on the floor beside her chair and picked it up. After rooting quickly through it, he brought out an amber plastic prescription bottle with a white safety cap and handed it to Crosby, saying, "This is it. This is all she takes, and it's never given her any trouble at all."

Crosby read the label on the bottle, shook her head, opened the cap, emptied a couple of pinkish capsules into her palm, smelled them, smelled the open bottle, put the capsules away, shut the bottle, and handed it back to Clement, saying, "No, not that. She doesn't take any tranquilizers, anything like that?"

"Aspirin, sometimes." Clement nervously rolled the prescription bottle in his hands. "Nothing else. Betsy and I do not believe in coddling ourselves."

Was he thinking about the array of patent medicines Jack French left behind on the bathroom counter?

Mort said, "What is it, Crosby? She's been poisoned?"

"Something in her system, yes," Crosby said. Clearly, she wasn't satisfied with her own diagnosis, didn't believe she completely understood the situation. She said, "It doesn't look like enough to kill her, but who knows."

Clement, who had been relaxing with the knowledge that Betsy wasn't dead, suddenly flared up again, shouting, "What? She's going to die?"

"I don't think so," Crosby told him, still being brisk and impersonal, "but who can say? I don't know what she's been given. Enough to knock her out, enough to lower her vital signs, but not enough—I *think* not enough—to put her away."

"Well, there must be something to *do*," Clement wailed, then leaned forward to call, "Betsy! Betsy!" The way he'd called Jack French down in the cocaine refinery.

"She can't hear you," Crosby said. "She's way down in there."

Mort said, "Crosby, you're sure this isn't a heart attack or something like that."

"Positive," she said. "Betsy was fed something. It looks like it wasn't enough to kill her, but close."

I said, "Fed something? During dinner, you mean?"

"I don't know," she said, spreading her hands in frustration. "Without knowing what it is, or how much she was given— I'd need a lab, and a lab technician, and a doctor, and a whole hospital. I'm just one little girl walking in her mama's footsteps."

"If it was put into something she ate," I suggested, "and if she didn't eat all of it, that might explain why she's still alive."

"If, and if," Crosby agreed. "I don't find any puncture wounds, needle marks, nothing like that, but it still could have been done that way. But I guess it's most likely something she ate or drank."

"So our murderer has come out in the open," Harriet said, sitting back in her chair again, fingers clasped together under her chin as she dispassionately gazed down at Betsy. She was seated, Crosby knelt on the floor, and the rest of us stood. Looking around at us all, Harriet said, "The first time, he tried but failed to imitate a suicide. The second time, he created an ambiguous disappearance. But this, this is poisoning and nothing else."

Was it the attack on Betsy that had finished the job of bringing Harriet back from her misery and grief? Probably so; her expression as she looked at each of us, firmly and quizzically meeting our eyes, was strong and self-assured. When her eyes met Danny's, he said, "I don't see what difference it makes, what point you're trying to make."

"You don't?"

"No," Danny said. "A faked suicide, a disappearance, a poisoning. It means he's adaptable, that's all, he takes advantage of his opportunities.''

"No, it means more than that," Harriet told him. "This is the end of ambiguity. I'm not sure what created the problem for him, but things have not gone right for our killer somehow, and he's become more desperate. This move he makes obvious and clear, not even trying to cover it up. That's the danger. He no longer cares for our good opinion.''

24

We carried Betsy up to the Hasbroucks' room and left her there, guarded by her husband. Crosby gave Clement a series of orders: Keep her warm. Don't try to give her anything to eat or drink. Don't fuss over her or move her around a lot or shout into her ear. Report any change in her breathing or pulse or skin temperature or *anything* to Crosby at once. He nodded, looking scared and exhausted, agreeing to everything, and once we left the room he firmly locked the door behind us, with a loud rasping of the key in the lock.

The eight of us gathered again in the observation room, pulling chairs over to make a loose oval so we could all talk together. But nobody had anything to say at first, this latest development having created a great wave of depression in its wake—where *would* this thing end?—until Harriet, in her new firm voice, said, "Someone in this room is a maniac."

"But a sly one," I said.

"An extremely dangerous maniac," Harriet agreed.

"He has some purpose in all this, but it's not likely to be a purpose we'll understand much, once we've finally got him. It'll be a mad purpose."

"How *do* we get him, though," Bly asked, "without a sensible motive?"

"By dealing in facts," Harriet told her, "observable facts."

"There are none," Danny said.

"Of course there are," Harriet insisted.

Fred told her, "If you're talking about timetables and all that, who was where at what time and who else did you see, we've already done it with the broken radio and it doesn't work. Anybody could have poisoned Betsy's predinner drink, or any of the food she ate, or whatever she had to drink after dinner—"

"Coffee," Mort said. "Which I served her."

"And I must admit," Harriet said, "her coffee was close enough on that little table between us, and I might have dropped something into it myself. But this person isn't invisible; he has to have left traces *somewhere*."

"There are too many of us," Fred objected. "We move around from place to place, it's only natural. Nobody can keep an eye on everybody else twenty-four hours a day."

I said, "What it comes down to is, we all have to keep an eye on *ourselves* until the storm lets up and the police can get here and we can all get off this island."

Crosby said, "Can't be too soon for me."

"Nor me," Mort agreed, with an enigmatic and almost hostile look at Danny, who pointedly ignored him.

Fred turned to look at me, saying, "Sam, I think it's time you came out of the phone booth and revealed yourself."

I was the only one who knew what he meant, everybody else getting a bit pop-eyed, thinking Fred must have suddenly decided I was the murderer. I said, "No, don't, forget it. There's no point in it."

"No point in what?" Harriet demanded.

"You might as well," Fred told me. "The cat is out of the bag."

And it was too. I could see the curiosity in all those faces. Shaking my head in irritation, I said, "What Fred's talking about is I used to be a cop. Years ago on Long Island."

"A policeman?" Harriet stared at me in wide-eyed hope. "We have a policeman among us?"

"Not really," I said. "That's why I never mentioned it. I was just a uniformed patrolman in a prowl car for a year and a half, and a little MP experience in the army before that. But I was never a detective, I don't claim the expertise. I haven't wanted to play Packard here, and I certainly don't want to play Columbo."

Fred said, "But you do have the background, you have the training. If push comes to shove, you have the authority."

"What authority?" I demanded.

It was Danny who answered, saying, "The authority the group gives you. I didn't know you were once a cop, but I'm glad to hear it. No matter how low-level you were, or think you were, you still have more grounding in this sort of thing, in real-life terms, than the rest of us. I wish I'd known about this before. As of now, you're in charge."

I was annoyed, but I was stuck with it, I could see that. "In charge of what?" I demanded.

Danny grinned at me and spread his hands. "In charge of keeping the rest of us alive," he said.

25

I failed.

Mort Weinstein's body was found at six-forty next morning by George Noble, when he went into the kitchen to start breakfast. George closed off the kitchen and came upstairs to get me, since I was now the resident expert. Bly and I were both up, though bleary-eyed, having spent half the night in useless conversation about what was going on in this house, and George took me out to the head of the stairs to tell me in private what had happened. "Shit," I said.

"Looks like there was a fight, this time," George told me.

I opened the bedroom door and saw Bly standing in the middle of the room, so filled with curiosity she almost glowed with it, like a phosphorescent sea. "I'll be right back," I promised her, "and I'll answer every question when I get here." I closed the door on her opening mouth, and George and I went down to the kitchen together.

There was blood in a streak angling down across the white front of the refrigerator. A row of blood dots trailed over the butcher block work-island, leading nowhere. There was blood in a pool on the floor near the lavatory door, under and around the body. The blood on the refrigerator and counter was dry, but that on the floor was still soft. The body was cold, but not rigid. "An hour ago," I said, looking toward the kitchen clock. "Maybe less." The digital clock read 6:44.

George said, "I thought I was the first one up. Then I saw the stains."

"Doesn't Danny usually get up the same time as you?"

He shook his head. "It's me first. I make coffee for Danny and me, then I bring it to him, and he comes down to help with breakfast."

"Mort doesn't usually get up at five-thirty, does he?"

"No." George grinned. "He likes—" Then he stopped, and looked at the body, and sighed. "Oh, well," he said.

"He likes his sleep, you were going to say."

"Yes."

"What's going on?"

It was Danny, in gray robe and red slippers. George and I stepped back from the body, watching him, and Danny saw it lying there, and he said in a stricken, distant way, "Oh."

"George found him," I said. "Just now."

"Oh, no," Danny said, still with that faraway voice. "No, Jesus, no." Then he glared at me, in sudden fury. "Why *Mort,* for Christ's sake?"

"I don't know," I said. "Why any of them?"

"But Mort, we— I *need*—" He shook his head,

stared with strained intensity at the body, muttered, "It's no goddamn good, I should never have agreed— Jesus, he was right about this place!"

"He wasn't happy about owning it," I said. "I do know that."

He gave me a look that might have been merely impatient, or might have been scornful. "You don't begin to know the story," he said.

"I wonder what it has to do with what's going on here."

"Nothing," Danny snapped, and nodded at the corner, saying, "Is that the knife?"

I hadn't noticed it before, a large utility knife, smeared maroon, tossed on the floor in the corner. "I suppose it is," I said.

George went over toward it, but Danny said, "Don't touch it! There might be fingerprints."

"They won't help us even if there are," I said. "We have no way to raise them, and no way to take prints from the people in the house."

Pointing toward the floor beyond the counter, George said, "Bloody dishtowel there. He probably wiped things off."

I said, "Danny? Why would Mort come down here at five-thirty in the morning?"

"To talk to somebody," he said. "To have a glass of warm milk because he couldn't sleep. To have a cup of coffee because he was getting up early. Any reason, no reason. I don't know why." He looked with muted anger at the body, as though Mort were to blame for being dead. "I suppose we'll have to tell the others," he said. "But we don't have to show him like this."

"No, of course not."

"Can you and George take him down to the freezer? I'll clean up in here."

"Do you have a camera? The police will want pictures of the scene."

So Danny went away to get a camera, and George started coffee, and I examined the body more closely. Mort had been stabbed four times; once in the back, once in the upper left arm, and twice in the chest. It was one of the chest wounds that had struck a vital spot, suggesting that the killer had attacked first from behind, but ineffectively. Mort had turned, been cut on the arm while turning, and then finally had been brought down while facing his killer. The grimace on Mort's face, and the way the fingers of his right hand tensely gripped at nothing, showed the savagery of the attack and defense.

If only Mort had been just a little faster.

Danny came back with a Polaroid camera and I repositioned the body as it had been. George went away to get a blanket, and after Danny took half a dozen shots we rolled the body in it, and George and I carried it away and down the stairs into the basements. George went in front, carrying the feet, and switching on lights as we descended, the absolute blackness below seeming to recede reluctantly before the indirect fluorescents.

The air in the freezer was dry and icy cold, a foretaste of what Mort's corpse was now cooling toward. We put it on the floor near the wrapped package that had been Daphne, and started out, both of us silent, the cold in there already getting into our bones, but at the door I stopped and looked back, because something bothered me. Something was wrong in here.

George reached for the light switch. "Wait a second," I told him, and went back across the room, and looked at the stiff folds of the frozen blanket around Daphne. I was the one who had put that blanket back around her during the second search, and I hadn't left it looking quite like that. Very reluctant, having no idea what I was going to find, not wanting to have to be the one to do this, I bent and pulled the woody blanket back, and looked at Jack French, lying on his back on top of Daphne.

26

He was very dead. A wire hanger had been bent around his neck and the ends twisted and twisted until the hanger was so tight it almost disappeared into his flesh. An area of matted blood on the top right of his skull suggested he'd been clubbed first, then strangled while unconscious. His skin looked slack and puffy and wrinkled. The letters D and W had been etched into his forehead with a knifepoint. His right hand had been hacked off and was missing, the stump ragged and torn and gray.

George looked down at him and said, "Oh, Jesus, have mercy."

"He was supposed to be found," I said, not understanding anything. "This was meant to be the display, he was supposed to be found. That's why he put the initials in the bed."

"Sir?" George didn't know about the initials in Jack's bed, of course.

"Never mind. Let's get out of here."

I covered the pair of bodies as they had been and we left, switching off the light and shutting the door. I said, "George, we didn't see that in there."

"I truly *wish* I hadn't seen it," he said.

"We didn't see it. We're not going to say anything to the people upstairs."

He studied me, thinking that over. "You think you know who it is?"

"No. But this is the first time we know something that the killer doesn't. I want to keep it that way."

George and I went back upstairs. The kitchen had been cleaned, and Danny was just bringing eggs and bacon and butter out of the refrigerator. "The story's spreading," he told us. "Everybody's in the observation room."

I left George with Danny, and walked out the passageway past the dimly lit hunting prints, through the empty dining and living rooms, and out to the observation room, where not quite everybody was assembled, and where the day looked just a bit brighter, at last.

The storm wasn't over, not at all, but it was less. The surface of the sea was less wind-lashed, the cloud cover higher, the clouds themselves were paler and less turbulent. Maybe our isolation here on Munro's Island was finally coming to an end.

Bly and Harriet and Fred and Crosby made a tight tense conversational group over by the windows. I joined them, and Harriet said, "Tell us about it."

So I described what I'd found in the kitchen as methodically as I could, and when I finished, Harriet said, "Was he right-handed or left-handed?"

"Right-handed," I said without thinking, then realized I was right, and was surprised I'd known it. The strokes had descended leftward, meaning a right-handed thrust.

"Danny and Betsy are the only left-handers among us," Harriet said. It was the sort of thing she would know. "Though that doesn't necessarily mean anything."

"Well, it can't be Betsy," Crosby said, "that much is for sure."

I said, "You saw her this morning?"

"Yeah, but it wasn't easy." She managed to grin and look fierce at the same time. "Clement didn't want to let me in, but I said, I'm *going* in, that's my patient."

"Crosby takes after her mama," Fred explained.

Ignoring him, Crosby said, "I don't know what Betsy's got, but the sooner we get her to a hospital, the better."

I said, "She's worse today?"

"No, she's the same, just the same. She ought to either get better or get worse, but it isn't happening." She shook her head, baffled. "I wish I knew what she'd been given. What kind of poison just puts you down and holds you steady like that? She just lies there, fibrillating pulse, strained breathing, no change. Clement's the one that's getting worse."

I said, "How so?"

"Nervous, paranoid—"

"We're all paranoid by now," Bly said, "and we're right to be."

"But it's making him sick," Crosby said. "He was in his dressing gown, with a scarf wrapped around his neck, shivering like it was cold in there."

I said, "Does he know about Mort?"

"No." Crosby shook her head. "I didn't know it myself until I came on down here."

"I think he'd better be informed," I said. "I'll go up and talk to him."

"Tell him he should eat breakfast," Crosby urged me.

"I will," I promised, and went away upstairs, and knocked on the Hasbroucks' door.

Clement's voice, sounding very tense, came from within: "Who is it?"

"Sam."

"What do you want?"

"Open up, Clement, I want to talk to you."

"We can talk through the door."

"No, we can't," I said, getting annoyed. "I'm not going to stand here and shout. We've had another event."

"An event? What?"

I said nothing, just folded my arms and leaned against the wall beside the door, and waited. Out of the corner of my eye I saw the door to Jack French's room, on the other side of the fireplace, and it stood open. Hadn't we left that closed?

The key rasped in the lock of the Hasbroucks' door, and it opened very slightly. The room within was dark, shades pulled down and curtains closed across the windows. I could barely see Clement, who was fiddling with something on the other side of the door. "There," he said at last.

"Clement?"

"I've propped a chair against the door," he explained. He was a blurred figure in the darkness. "We can see each other, we can talk. Forgive me, Sam, but I'm just not secure enough as yet in my own ratiocinations. If I am right in what I suspect, then you are as innocent as I. But what if I am wrong?"

"You suspect someone?"

"I'm not quite ready to lay an accusation at any particular doorstep," he told me. His voice trembled and his hand kept fidgeting with the knob, rattling it. "Soon, perhaps. You say there has been another event?"

"Mort Weinstein was murdered this morning, in the kitchen."

"Mort!" But Clement didn't sound surprised, he sounded triumphant, as though this proved some theory he'd been developing. In confirmation of that idea, he said, "So, we are in endgame at last!"

"The storm is lessening, if that's what you mean."

"Not quite," he said. His eyes glinted in the darkness. "If I am correct, our particular indoor storm may be completely finished now."

"I hope you're right, then," I told him.

"As do I, Sam, as do I."

"Crosby says you should come down for breakfast."

"*Oh*, no," he said, receding farther into the dimness in the room. "And leave Betsy here, so he can finish the job? Besides, I'm too close to him now, Sam. What if he suspects how close I am?"

"We're all together downstairs," I told him. "We're safer as a group."

"Was Betsy safer?" His voice broke on the name. "No, Sam. Until I know for certain, I shall not leave this room."

"What about food? You can't possibly—"

"Oh, but I can. And I will. Do you think I *dare* to eat, as things are?"

There was going to be no swaying him, I could see that. It was in his nature to be melodramatic as hell anyway, and given the circumstances, including Betsy

in some sort of coma, I could hardly tell him he was
wrong. "All right," I said, then glanced again at the
open door beyond the fireplace. "Clement, wasn't Jack's
door closed?"

"Of course it was," he said.

"Well, it isn't now."

I moved away from Clement and over to that other
door, and looked in at a room that at first seemed
exactly as I'd last seen it, when we'd searched and
found the initials in the bed, left by an angry and
bewildered murderer, scrambling to get his scheme back
on track. But then I saw the sheet of paper taped to the
window. "Ah," I said.

Clement had leaned very slightly out of his own
doorway, his head barely visible beyond the fireplace.
He called, "What is it?"

"A note," I said, and went into Jack's room and
crossed to the window.

The note was on a sheet torn out of the memo pad I'd
seen atop the dresser in here the last time. The words
were small and crabbed and written in green ink, slant-
ing across the page.

There was a clicking sound behind me. I turned and
saw the bathroom door open, Clement having just unlocked the bolt on the inside. He peered around the edge
of the door at me. He was, as Crosby had said, in his
dressing gown, with a black scarf tucked in under the
lapels. He said, "What is it?"

I read the note aloud:

> "Stupid amateurs. By the time a real cop
> gets here, I'll be finished with all of you."

Half-whispering, Clement said, "From *Jack*?"

"It isn't signed."

I crossed the room to pick up the cancer-spot script from the bedside table, Clement recoiling into the bathroom as I did so, then hesitantly easing the door open again to watch. I carried the script back over to the note on the window and compared the gnarly writing on the one with the gnarly writing on the other, both in the same green ink. "Well, what do you know," I said. "It's the same handwriting."

27

"**I** don't know why I should feel better," Bly said, "and yet I do."

We were in the observation room again, after breakfast, standing near an outer corner, in an L of windows showing the steadily brightening day. Danny and George had arranged a breakfast exclusively from communal servers—a large common bowl of scrambled eggs, a platter of bacon, a big jug of coffee, a wooden board stacked with toast—and we had eaten it together, all of us except Clement and Betsy, with the assurance that the killer couldn't poison one of us without poisoning all, including himself. "If you feel better," I suggested to Bly, "maybe it's because you had a big breakfast."

"But we're still here in this house," she pointed out, "and nothing has changed, really."

"The storm is going away," I said, nodding at it. "Heading north at last."

She looked out the window, giving the storm an ironic look. "It's still taking its time," she said. "It'll be tomorrow anyway before it's gone and a plane can fly in.'' She shivered theatrically. ''Another night in this place.''

''And yet you feel better.''

''I do. I feel as though the worst is over. Why is that?''

''Beats me,'' I said.

Bly stretched, grinning at me. ''Maybe it's because I had a good long hot shower this morning after you went away with George. I was afraid, after yesterday, we were going to have constant trouble about the hot water, and I'd *hate* that.''

''I think yesterday everybody must have decided to take their baths and showers at the same time.''

''Mort said that was just one thing about the place that didn't live up to its promise,'' she said. ''I asked him about it yesterday, and he said there was supposed to be a great big water heater in the basement that would *never* run out, but the first time they have a group of people here, look what happens. More expense replacing it, he said. He didn't like this house much, you know, even before everything that happened. Poor Mort, dead in a house he hated.''

''You know,'' I said, ''Clement seems to feel the same way as you right now. You say you just have this feeling the worst is over, and Clement said, 'We're in endgame at last.' As though there's some sense in the air that the killer had this long and complicated scheme in his mind, and now it's worked out to the finish, and unless something goes drastically wrong, the rest of us aren't in danger anymore.''

''That *is* the way I feel,'' Bly agreed. ''But there's no sense in it. *Why* feel that way?''

"Now that Mort is dead."

"Exactly." Bly frowned out at the frothing gray sea and the high dirty-white clouds. "Why should Mort's death feel like the end of something? Why should the killer stop there? Why wouldn't he be planning to get rid of us all? He's already killed three people, if Jack French is really dead, or four if you count the pilot, and he almost killed Betsy."

"Jack's dead, all right," I said. I hadn't yet had a chance to take her aside and tell her about my discovery down in the freezer. "So he's had four victims, not counting the pilot. And the pilot *doesn't* count; that was definitely an accident."

"So he started with Daphne," Bly said, "and then Jack, and then Betsy, and then Mort. Is that a progression? Before we came here, what did those four have in common? Who even knew them all?"

"Nobody."

"So it's *random,* it has to be, so why—"

"Oh," I said, because I suddenly understood something. "Oh, like *that.*"

Bly gave me a sudden sharp look. "You figured it out? You know who the murderer is?"

"No," I said. "But I do know something else, at last." I looked around, and Fred and Crosby were at the backgammon table again, playing with fierce comedy. Taking Bly's arm, I said, "Go over there and challenge the winner."

"Fred, you mean."

"Yes. But beat him, Bly, knock him out of the box. I want the chance to take Fred away for a little discreet conversation."

28

She did beat him, too, and at the end he gave her a look of smiling and surprised respect, saying, "You're tough when you want to be, aren't you?"

"Yes," Bly said simply.

Getting to his feet, making way for Crosby at the board, Fred looked over at me and said, "You're next at bat, are you?"

"Sure."

"Then me," he said. "I'll want my revenge."

"While we're waiting," I said to him, "come over here and let's talk."

"When wise man wishes to talk," said his Charlie Chan, "other wise men listen." And he followed me down the length of the room, past Harriet reading, past George fiddling morosely with the radio, past Danny frowning as he did some sort of accounts in a ledger book. Down by the elevator, with the white sky beyond the windows making us all look like silhouettes, I turned and said, "I want to keep this just between us for a while."

"Whatever you say. What's up?"

I leaned close, bending down toward his open friendly face, saying confidentially, "I found Jack."

"No!" Excitement shone in his eyes. With a quick look around to be sure no one was listening, he put a hand on my forearm and half-whispered, "Where?"

"Where you put him."

He looked at me with a leftover smile still tacked more or less in place. A little silence stretched between us as we both waited for him to decide whether or not it was worth trying a bluff. Then all at once the tired old smile was replaced by a bright new one, an impish grin, and he said, "Pretty good. How'd you figure out where it was?"

"I didn't," I admitted. "But George and I carried Mort downstairs this morning, and I saw there was something different."

"Ah," he said. "Blind luck. Not much I can do about that."

"No, not much. Then Bly told me she talked with Mort yesterday about hot water, and how he said there was supposed to be a steady supply—"

"That *was* the tricky part," he agreed.

"So you stashed him in the water heater until—"

"No no no," he said, waving his hands to stop me, wanting me to get it right. "Didn't you go down there to see what we did?"

"No. I just figured this part out a couple minutes ago."

"Okay," he said. "What you've got down there is a kind of two-step operation. There's a fairly small electric hot water heater, but then beyond that there's like a great big holding tank with its own heater to maintain the temperature. The water heater's sealed, but the holding tank has a round cover on top, so you can get in to clean it. We turned off the heat on the holding tank, opened one valve and shut another valve so the hot water supply bypassed it and came straight up from the hot water heater, then drained the tank, put Jack in it, and filled it with cold water. Did you people look in there during the second search?''

"No."

"Well, you wouldn't have seen him," he said. "The only problem was, too many people were using hot water, more than the heater could keep up with, and we couldn't get back right away. Crosby and I had to pretend we were sleepy, go up to the room, wait for everybody else to settle down, then sneak down to the basement and move Jack and drain the holding tank all over again. *Then* we could switch back to the normal hot water supply.''

"Fred," I said, "do you mind telling me why you went to all the trouble?''

"We didn't like the setup," he told me. Looking out the window at passing squalls, he said, "If you'd seen Jack, you'd know what I mean.''

"I wish I had seen him.''

"Maybe not. The thing is," Fred explained, "he was *meant* to be found. It was supposed to be a shocker, to throw us all for a loop. Crosby and I looked at it, and thought it over, and decided we didn't want to play his game, we didn't want to be the patsies who come running upstairs and yell, 'Look what *we* found!' The whole thing was so elaborate, you know? So what we figured was, if we change the script on him, maybe it'll throw him off balance, maybe he'll stumble and do something that exposes him. But all he did was that weird set of initials in the bed." Shaking his head, he said, "I don't follow this guy's mind, I really don't."

"Tell me how Jack was when you found him."

"Well, first it was his hand," Fred told me. "We went into the armory room, and the hand was on the floor by itself, palm up, fingers half-curled like it was beckoning to us to come a little closer. There was a big X of blood on the floor, and the hand was in the middle of it."

"And the window?"

"Closed. We opened it when we cleaned the floor with a rag we found in the laboratory. We got the rag wet from the rain outside, then threw it out the window when we were done."

"All right. Where was the rest of the body?"

"Down in the dungeon, at the bottom of the basements, naked, lying on the floor on his back, with a rope around his neck tied to that iron ring in the floor."

"Very melodramatic," I suggested.

"If offended us," Fred told me, then grinned at himself and shrugged, saying, "I know it sounds weird, but it didn't shock us or scare us or do anything it was supposed to do; it just irritated us. As though we were being condescended to, you know? He was playing down to us."

"He was insulting your intelligence."

"That's exactly right," Fred said. "And we just didn't want to have to play it the way he set it up. It was Crosby's idea to cross him up, hide the body, clean up the armory, and I went along with her a hundred percent. In fact, she was the one did most of it, with me saying, 'Honey, I think I'm gonna throw up,' and her saying, 'Pick up that foot and be quiet.' "

"And the hand?"

Again he shrugged. "Out the window." Then, cocking his head quizzically, looking up at me, he said, "It occurs to me, you coming to have a quiet little chat like this, it means you know I hid the body but you don't think I'm the killer."

"That's right. Once I doped it out there were *two* people involved in Jack's disappearance, and the one who murdered him was not the same as the one who put him in the freezer, then I saw how it had to have happened, that you and Crosby had found him the first time through, hid him somewhere, then went back later and moved him to the freezer. His skin is all puffy, like a white prune, so that suggested he'd been in water for a while. Bly talked about the lack of hot water, and there it was."

"Elementary, my dear Holt."

"The question is," I said, "what next. I assume, by the way, that you realize I'm not the murderer either, or I would have had a different reaction when I figured out you were the guy who spoiled my dramatic scene."

"It's hard to cross people off the list," he said, "because there's so few of us. You and Bly, Harriet and Clement, that's about it. Which makes the killer either Danny or George, so then I start thinking about Harriet and Clement again, and then I start thinking about you again, and around it goes. Do you want to tell everybody else about Jack?"

"No, I don't," I said. "I want to keep to myself *every* secret I might know."

"Oh." He looked very interested. "You mean there might be other things, and you're not telling me?"

I thought of the note on Jack's window, which only Clement and I so far knew about. "Yes," I said.

He waited, then laughed and looked away. "Ah," he said, "Bly's finished with Crosby. Come on along, she wants to hand *you* your head now, with all its little secrets still inside."

29

Bly whipped me handily, and then Fred took my place, avidly rubbing his hands together and saying in his father's Japanese-interrogator voice, "So, American spy, you think you understand this game."

"Try me, Tojo," Bly snapped.

I strolled away from the game, and Harriet looked up from her reading to say, "Sit down a minute, Sam. I may call you Sam?"

"Of course," I said, taking the chair next to her, where Betsy had been sitting last night when she collapsed.

"I've had a lot of time to think these last two days," Harriet said with a little grimace of irony. "And my primary conclusion is that I'm not as damn smart as I think I am."

"Oh? Why's that?"

"Miss Marple. I have no idea, of course," she said, "what your relationship is with that Packard character of yours."

187

"I'm trying to divorce him," I said.

She nodded, with a sidelong look and smile. "Probably sensible, all in all. As for me, although I've never subsumed myself within the Miss Marple character, as for instance Clement has done with Sherlock Holmes—"

"It would be hard to match Clement," I agreed.

"Nevertheless," she said, "unconsciously I have been identifying myself with that character, as though I did have her insights and her view of life. For instance, Fred pokes fun at his Charlie Chan character, a thing I would not have done. Without realizing it, I would think that I was poking fun at myself."

"It's hard to keep the identities separate," I said. "I agree with that."

"And so, without giving it much thought, one begins to think that one can do what one's character does. One begins to *expect* it of oneself."

I smiled, remembering my occasional fantasy that I can pilot a plane. "I know exactly what you mean," I said.

"Yes, I'm sure you do." She gave me a level look, and said, "But here's the other part of it. I thought my view of death and of murder must be like Miss Marple's as well, but I find that it is not."

"Ah."

"To Miss Marple, violent death is merely untidy, and the finding of its cause constitutes a kind of tidying up. The view is bloodless and detached. I have never been close to actual murder before, and therefore never had to take a critical look at that view, compare it with my own."

"No, I suppose not."

"The death of Daphne," Harriet said with a long

wavering sigh, as she gazed sternly away out the window, "has drastically changed my life. The rest of it I don't care about, Mort Weinstein or Jack French, if he's dead, or the pilot, whatever his name was, if he actually was sabotaged, which I don't in fact believe."

"Neither do I."

"But I don't *care* about them," she said, "I'm not interested in *solving* anything, and I don't much care, on the intellectual side, if anyone else solves anything. If it's all untidy, it doesn't matter to me, because it's not *my* untidiness. And as for Daphne, that is not untidiness, not mere untidiness, that is the end of my life as well, a life that I led and was comfortable with and cared about. Daphne could be difficult—you saw that at the final dinner—I nearly said the last supper." She laughed at herself, not because anything was funny but because she had to pull back from the brink of too much emotion. She wanted to talk this out, but it was dangerous for her, so now she had to move back from it briefly.

I said, "A longtime couple is a complicated machine, I know that. Usually, the rest of the world just sees the dull bits or the difficult bits."

She smiled gratefully, saying, "Yes, that's true. We were a complicated machine, and now I'm just an inert machine *part,* like those toothed cams and things you see in an alley behind a factory. Right now it seems to me very unlikely *this* old rusty part will ever be found useful in a functioning machine again."

"I don't think anybody can ever say that for sure," I said, which was as far as I wanted to go along those lines. The fact was, Harriet was famous, she was fairly powerful and widely well thought of, and if she wasn't actually rich, she was damn close. Replacing Daphne would not be at all impossible, if that's what she wanted, nowhere near as difficult as it would be for someone who was poor and powerless and unknown. And she was strong as well, so she wasn't likely to repine and grieve forever. At this moment, though, to point all that out might seem cynical or unfeeling, so I simply made a conventional noise in the conventional place, and let her get on with it.

Which she did. "Whatever may happen in the future," she began, meaning she'd already thought out for herself everything I'd just decided not to say, "at the moment, my concentration is on what has happened now, the devastation that has just happened right now."

"Of course," I said. "It would have to be."

"And so I've learned another difference between Miss Marple and me," she said. "I don't want to solve the murder, I don't want to tidy up the untidiness, I don't want to engage in an intellectual contest. I care too much about Daphne and too little about the others." She leaned closer, her cold gray eyes looking into mine, her voice dropping as she said, calmly and seriously, "I want to commit a murder."

I didn't know how to react to that. Was it supposed to be funny? Was it unintentionally funny? Could she actually mean it? And even if she did, was it something I could take seriously? I just met her gaze, keeping my own expression blank, and waited for her to continue.

The pause probably seemed longer than it was, and then she said, "You do understand that, don't you?"

"I'm not sure," I said carefully. "Revenge, you mean?"

"In a way, I suppose." She nodded, thinking that

over. "But not in the way you might think," she added. "I don't want to kill him as a simple tit for tat, an eye for an eye, you killed Daphne so now I kill you. That's stupid, that's politicians and religious fanatics. What I want is something different from that, and simpler, and cleaner. I want to keep him from being taken seriously."

I shook my head. "I'm sorry, I don't follow."

"The storm is ending," she pointed out with a nod at the windows.

"Moving north."

"Ending for us, then. The police will come here. There are too few of us and too many events have occurred, so there will be cracks in the scheme. The police will investigate, they'll question us, they'll have laboratory tests they can perform, you know all these things better than I do—"

"They'll get him, in other words," I said.

"Oh, yes, of course they'll get him. It's only his madness that makes him think otherwise. They'll get him, I'm sure, with no trouble at all. Or her, since it is still possibly a woman."

"Possibly."

"But then," she said, "they'll fly him away to the mainland and give him psychiatric examinations, and the newspapers will be full of headlines about him, and his picture will be on television, and he will be treated as a very important and interesting celebrity for a while. And even more so if it turns out to be a woman."

"That's all true," I admitted. "But only for a few months. And then the trial—"

"Commitment, I should think," she corrected me, "as he or she certainly *is* mad. In any event, whatever jurisdiction we eventually turn out to be in, whatever set of laws our murderer will face, the death penalty is extremely unlikely. So, whether it's commitment or a trial, at the end of it there he'll be, or there she will be, warm and cozy, with a lovely scrapbook of clippings. And here I'll be, without Daphne.''

"I see what you mean.''

"It's more than unfair,'' she said. "Because, no matter what, he's going to win. Or she's going to win. It doesn't matter if that person is caught or not, he's won already. So that's why I would like to murder him—or her—myself. I just see that gloating figure, in a comfortable little room somewhere, not even a cell really, leafing through the scrapbook. I'd like to remove that vision both from my imagination and from reality.''

"I can see why you would.''

"So there's another difference between Miss Marple and myself,'' Harriet said with a very cold smile. "She wants to solve murders and tidy up. I want to commit a murder. That's *my* kind of tidying up.''

30

Lunch was again a communal meal, none of us eating anything that didn't come from a common pot. There was a green pea soup, there were jugs of tea and coffee, and a loaf of bread from which each of us sliced what we wanted. (The bread knife Danny supplied was barely big enough for the job, but nobody made any jokes about it.)

It was a very quiet meal; hard to believe seven people could be that silent. From time to time, I'd look up and see people gazing speculatively at this person or that person, but they'd always soon duck their heads down again and stare into their soup, afraid to make eye contact.

Harriet. Danny. George. Fred. Crosby. Bly. Me. Upstairs, Clement and Betsy. We all knew this sequence of events was coming to an end, that people would arrive from the mainland either late today or, more likely, tomorrow morning. At that point, the murderer among us would meet his final test, and either pass or fail. How had he survived this long? Was there a chance, despite Harriet's statements of assurance a little while ago, was there a chance at all that he *wouldn't* be caught, not by us, not by the police, not ever?

I think that's what we must all have been brooding about during lunch; all but one of us, of course. Earlier convictions—well, it couldn't be him, it couldn't be her—were being swept away. It could be anybody. Fred's game with Jack French's corpse, for instance, could have been deeper than it seemed; and when you stopped to think about it, how improbable it was to react in the way he claimed. We were all, it's true, gaited more than the usual toward the dramatic and the melodramatic, it wasn't confined to Clement, who was merely the most extreme example of our shared tendency. But if Fred and Crosby had *not* killed Jack, how could they so casually have tossed his remains about like that? Could Fred's determination not to let someone else upstage him, not to become a minor role in somebody else's Grand Guignol production, really have been that strong?

Then there was Harriet. The murderer, now that we were moving into what Clement had called endgame, must be getting more and more nervous, must be wanting to add just a bit of icing to the cake, give the clay mold just one more pat. Had Harriet in reality found it necessary herself to get rid of Daphne, and had everything else followed from that, and was she now pressing the fact of her pseudo-widowhood to divert suspicion?

It went on like that, and I'm sure much the same thing was happening in every other brain at the table. But when I found myself at last wondering what I really knew about Bly Quinn—whose one published book, the collection of short stories, was after all titled *Hesitation Cuts*—I suddenly realized I'd gone overboard and was ceasing to make any kind of sense at all. And was everybody else at the table going similarly bananas? The silence continued.

It was broken by Crosby, at the end of the meal, who suddenly spoke up, saying, "George, let me have a tray and two clean bowls and two spoons."

"Sure thing," George said without question, and got up from the table to go into the kitchen, while Danny said, "Crosby? What's that for?"

"Clement doesn't know it yet," Crosby told him with determination, "but he's about to eat lunch. I'll be his taster, he can see for himself everything's okay. I just simply can't leave that man up there like that."

George brought the tray and the bowls and the spoons, and Crosby added to it the third-full pot of soup and a thick slab of bread, but not the knife. It all made for a large and heavy load on the tray, but when Fred volunteered to carry it up for her, Crosby said, "*Oh,* no. He sees an army coming, he'll *nail* the door shut." She picked up the tray and marched off with it.

Fred looked around the table at the rest of us. "If everybody doesn't mind," he said, "while Crosby's off by herself like that, let's all the rest of us stick together."

No one minded. There were only six of us in the dining room now, so we all carried the remains of lunch to the kitchen and got in one another's way there, doing the washing up and putting everything away. Fred asked me for a description of what I'd found when George had called me to the kitchen this morning, and I obliged, pointing out where and how Mort had been lying, and the position of the bloodstains. "He fought," Fred said, nodding at the scrubbed-clean places. "Or at least he tried to fight. It's too bad he didn't at least mark the fella, give him a black eye or something."

"I had the exact same thought this morning," I said.

In a body we trooped back to the observation room, past the hunting prints and the cold-looking dining room and the sprawling empty living room with its puffy low-slung furniture, like an African hunting lodge or old-fashioned hotel lobby. In the observation room, Fred and Bly made for the backgammon board, Harriet to her book, George to the radio, and I to the windows, to consider the storm.

The rain had virtually stopped, it seemed now little more than windblown spume. The clouds were higher and a very glary white, almost luminescent. The white-caps on the black sea were smaller, crinkly, in long rows, like the ocean in a bad painting.

Danny had gone to the bar to make himself a drink, and now he joined me, nervously shaking ice in a glass that seemed to contain mostly vodka. "Tomorrow morning," he said, looking out.

"Probably. Not today, though."

"In a way," Danny said, and paused to sip at his drink, and started again. "In a way, I'm sorry it's coming to an end. Scared, in fact."

I stared at him. That was the last reaction I would have expected from anybody at all in this house. "Sorry it's *ending*?" I asked him. "Scared?"

"Now I am," he explained. "Since Mort died. Or since he was the last to die, put it that way."

"If he is the last."

Danny grinned, a quick nervous flicker like summer lightning. "Oh, we're finally taking precautions, aren't we? Hanging out together, all of that. I don't see any-body else getting it, do you?"

"Probably not."

"So that makes Mort the last, and that's bad news for me. Because when it comes to Mort, I have a motive."

I was surprised, and it probably showed. I'm not *that* good an actor. "You have a motive?"

"Money. The best motive there is."

"You mean, there's some kind of financial troubles with Danmor Forever?"

"Legal financial troubles." He gave me a quick bitter look, almost as though his troubles were somehow my fault, and said, "I wouldn't tell you this, but it's going to come out now, anyway. No choice anymore."

"Because of Mort's death."

"That's right. We're being taken to court by a couple of our series stars for shortchanging them on the profit percentages."

"That's happened before," I said.

"These people have the goods on us," Danny told me. "Or, that is, on *me*. Mort was never a party to it. We had a partnership of— Well, he was Mr. Inside, I was Mr. Outside. He did the technical stuff, the produc-tion stuff. I made the deals and schmoozed the people. I didn't know much what he was doing, and he didn't know much what I was doing. There's a *lot* Mort didn't know about, and I think he was basically happier that way. I know he was goddamn unhappy about the money thing."

"Did he tell people so?"

"Our lawyers," Danny said. "And at least one of the people we were screwing. The thing is, if we were all to stick together and stonewall, then it stays a civil suit, we argue a while, we settle out of court, life goes on. But Mort was talking about breaking ranks. He hadn't been in on it, he hadn't profited from it, he didn't want any part of it, and he was thinking about pulling the plug.''

"Which would mean what?"

"Well, maybe jail for me," Danny said. "Bankruptcy, anyway. The end of the production company, with Mort smelling like a rose, all the contract people still with him because he's such a wonderful guy, and me outside in the cold." The quick bitter grin flashed again. "I don't care if I *am* the villain," he said, "I still don't particularly want to get what I've got coming to me."

"It hadn't been resolved yet? Mort hadn't made up his mind whether to stick with you or not?"

"No, not yet. And this goddamn house wasn't helping. *I* was the one forced it down his throat, for reasons of my own, and he didn't like it from the beginning. Once your crowd showed up, and the storm, and Ralph McCloskey getting wasted like that, and then all this lunacy, well, that's all Mort needed. *Everything* was getting to be my fault. I was hoping he'd calm down once this nightmare was over and we were back in L.A., but who knows? And now he's dead, and what does that make me?"

"The prime suspect," I suggested. "Of course, there were other killings before."

"Decoys, or false trails, or coverups, or who knows what." He shrugged. "The only hope I have left," he said, "is that Jack French really is still alive somewhere in this house, because if he is, then *he's* the prime suspect."

"He isn't," I said.

Danny gave me a quick keen look, his pale eyebrows lowering. "You know this for certain?"

"Yes."

"Because you killed him, or for other reasons?"

"Other reasons."

"Then I'm in trouble." He gazed out the window, slowly nodding. "I've been rooting for Jack French," he said. "A bad guy, a drunk, already had trouble with the law, probably a little crazy before he ever got here. I've been trying not to think about the whole mess, except it should be Jack French, to get me off the hook. And now you tell me it isn't."

"Sorry."

"Not your fault," he said.

Movement made me turn my head, and Crosby was just coming back into the room. She looked around, saw us, and headed in our direction.

Danny all at once gave a surprised and bitter chuckle, looking out at the windswept sea as though he could read messages in the shapes of the waves. "Jesus Christ," he said. "I probably even know who it is. Not that *that* would do me any good."

"The killer? Who?"

"My lips are sealed," he said with a sardonic side-long glance. "Believe me, believe me it wouldn't do me any good. Besides, I'm probably wrong *again*."

Crosby joined us at the window, saying, "By golly, it's almost a nice day. Anybody for the beach?"

"Not quite yet," I said.

To Danny, Crosby said, "Clement says he'd like to talk to you. He actually did say, 'At his convenience.' And bowed, like this." She bowed stiffly.

"Sure, at my convenience." Everything was making

Danny bitter by now. He acted as though the summons were not a surprise, and not a pleasure. Grinning crookedly at me, he said, "Maybe I should have been a good boy, after all. But who knew?"

He went away, leaving the observation room, and Crosby looked after him, saying, "What was that all about?"

"Chickens coming home to roost." Looking through the living room doorway, I could see Danny heading for the stairs to his own tower, not the guest tower. I turned to Crosby: "Did Clement eat?"

"Like a horse. He's a lot calmer too."

"That's good."

"The one that worries me is Betsy," she said. "Still no change in her. She just lies there, out of it, pulse and breathing both shaky but not getting worse. How long can she go on like that?"

"I have no idea," I said. "But we'll be able to get her to a hospital tomorrow."

She nodded at the weather. "Looking up." Still gazing outward, she said, "Clement says he's solved our little crime wave."

"He has?" First Danny, now Clement.

"So he says. He says he'll make his announcement at dinner tonight."

"By emissary, or does he intend to come down himself?"

"Oh, he'll come down to dinner," Crosby said, "first carefully locking Betsy in the room so nobody can get at her. But Clement wants to do his act to a full house."

"Well, I'll be there," I said. Through the doorway, I

saw Danny come down from his tower and head for Clement, moving briskly.

"Me, too," Crosby told me. "Wouldn't miss it for the world."

31

Backgammon had begun to pall. Now that Bly had found her stride, the game had become simply a seesaw battle between her and Fred, with Crosby and me occasionally climbing aboard for comic relief. I accepted the humiliation a couple of times and then decided I'd had enough, and wandered over to watch George poke aimlessly among the radio parts as though he were reading entrails. He looked up when I arrived, gave me a sad smile and a shake of the head, and said, "It is hopeless, you know."

"I know."

"But I keep trying." He sighed. "I want to hear my Blondel."

"I'm sure you do." I sat at the table across from him. "We'll be out of here by tomorrow morning."

He glanced over at the windows. "Yes. Not today, though."

"No."

He frowned at the disassembled radio once more,

then switched the frown to me, saying, "Why did your lady say to me before, 'The flight of the phoenix'?"

I couldn't help laughing. "Things remind Bly of other things," I said. "That was a movie about a group of people in a plane crash in the desert. One of them is a professional model-airplane designer, and he leads the rest in building a new airplane out of the parts of the old one, and they fly out to safety at the end."

"Ah, I see." He gestured at the radio pieces. "The phoenix."

"Yes."

"But this one doesn't rise from its ashes."

"I don't think so, no."

He poked a bit at a couple of the parts, then frowned at me again, saying, "So you're a policeman."

"Not anymore."

"But you were."

"Yes."

He nodded, very somber and serious, and then said, "What do you think my chances are?"

I didn't know what he was talking about, and said so: "What chances?"

"With the police. They will think I'm the guilty one, won't they?"

I was astonished. "Why on earth should they?"

"Well," he said, being calm and reasonable, "I am the black man. And although I am not the butler, I am a servant. And I am the only person here who knew everyone who was attacked."

"Daphne and Jack you met in Jamaica, you mean."

"Yes. And Mr. Weinstein was my boss's partner. And of course I knew Ralph, the pilot."

"But there's Betsy Hasbrouck," I said. "She's still alive, but she was attacked."

"But I knew her," he said, as though I should have known that.

More astonishment. I said, "You knew her? Before she came here? How?"

"When I worked for Danny in Los Angeles," he said, "oh, five or six years ago, he loaned me to Mrs. Hasbrouck a few times."

"*Loaned* you?"

"Yes." He smiled at my confusion and said, "Let me explain. I went to work for Danny as a houseman, very simple tasks, but the cook was a very bad woman, bad-tempered and drunk sometimes, and Danny didn't like her."

"Danny's a good cook himself."

"Oh, yes. And he saw I was interested, so he taught me to cook, and we cooked together sometimes, and finally he fired the cook and put me in that job. And sometimes he would loan me to friends of his, especially to do Caribbean cooking, and they would pay me extra. And that's how I met Mrs. Hasbrouck. When Danny loaned me to her, she would work with me in the kitchen because she wanted to learn how to do the things."

"I didn't know Danny and the Hasbroucks were social friends," I said.

"Oh, I don't think they were," he told me, shaking his head. "Maybe just business friends. I never saw the Hasbroucks at any of Danny's parties."

I said, "You've worked for Danny a long time, then."

"About three years," he said. "Then I went back to Jamaica and became a married man."

"And worked as a bartender."

"And cook," he said. "And so on."

"And now you're back with Danny again."

"Oh, only temporarily," he said with a certain emphasis, as though dissociating himself from an ongoing relationship with Danny. "I needed the money, you see," he went on, "because of the baby coming. And I had only a substitute's job, so I couldn't very well say no."

I said, "You would have preferred to say no?"

Instead of answering that, he said, "When they have the filming facilities all ready here, they will have a complete staff then, all sorts of people. Danny just asked me to come for a little while at the beginning. He offered a great amount of money. And I am grateful to him, he taught me a great deal when I worked for him before."

George's evasion of my question, combined with his obvious feeling that he had to justify and explain why he would work for Danny Douglas at all, prodded at my curiosity. I said, "What was it that made you quit working for him before, in Los Angeles?"

"Oh, well," he said. "It was time to go home, I think, home to Jamaica."

"George," I said, putting more force into it, "did it have anything to do with drugs?"

He didn't look frightened, merely very troubled. He watched the broad tips of his fingers randomly move radio parts this way and that on the table. "Always a lot of drugs around Los Angeles," he said.

I waited, watching him.

He glanced over at the windows, as though he might change the subject back to the weather, then snuck a look at me to see if I was still waiting, then gazed vaguely around the room, then shrugged and faced me directly and said, "I never had anything to do with drugs. Not me. I don't like that business."

"Is that why you left?"

"I wasn't happy in Los Angeles," he said stubbornly.

Was that all I was going to get out of him? Well, it was enough anyway; a vague idea I'd been forming was now confirmed. "Okay, George," I said.

He pushed back from the table, his expression strained and discontented, as though he had at last been given permission to leave a difficult interview. "I should begin to think about dinner," he said, though it was far too early for that.

I rose, saying, "That's all right, George, I won't pester you anymore."

"Oh, no, no," he said, also rising, looking up at me with an attempt at open innocence. "Not pestering me at all. I did start it, I asked you about the police."

"Well, the answer to that," I told him, feeling obscurely that I owed him some sort of reassurance, "is that the police will get to the bottom of things here. It'll take more than skin color and cooking with Betsy Hasbrouck in Los Angeles to get you convicted of anything."

He smiled at me, suddenly cheerful. "All I want, you know," he said, "is to go home and see my Blondel and my new baby. And forget this place entirely and forever."

"Amen to that," I said, and movement at the door attracted my attention. I looked that way, and here came

Clement, striding in, a small notebook clasped to his heart.

He stopped and looked around, the chiseled features at their most patrician over the black cashmere scarf. "If I may have your attention," he said unnecessarily.

32

We gathered around him like first-graders around the teacher at story time, and he accepted us in the same fashion, nodding as we took our places, gesturing with his long-fingered hand for us to find chairs and settle ourselves.

He himself remained on his feet. His manner was solemn, almost priestly. If he was being theatrical—well, of course he was being theatrical—it was in the most dignified and elegant manner imaginable.

Did Harriet try to take him down a peg? I'm not sure, but her tone was suspiciously matter-of-fact when she said, "Crosby told us all you had a major pronouncement to make at dinnertime. Is this it, or is this something else?"

"This is it," he told her with a faint smile, as though to say nothing could ruffle his composure now; not now. "When I spoke to Crosby," he went on, "when in fact I suggested to Crosby that I had solved our little mystery here, and that I would be presenting my solution at dinnertime, I knew I was being premature, that I wasn't then quite ready to present my ideas, but I confess to a certain excitement at knowing I was so close, and I did believe I would have the last pieces of the puzzle firmly in place when the moment came. As it turned out, however, the final elements arrived sooner than I had anticipated. Knowing the tension we have all been suffering these last two days, I felt it would be grossly unfair to permit that uncertainty to cloud us all an instant longer than necessary. That is why, with your permission, I would like to present my conclusions now for your consideration, rather than wait." He looked around, smiling and nodding. "We are all here," he said, "and if there's no objection I'll—"

"Danny," Fred said. "Danny isn't here."

"I will come to that," Clement told him, dismissing the issue gently but firmly.

I said, "He went up to talk to you. You asked to see him."

"As I say, Sam," he told me, "we will come to that. All in good time."

This was, in other words, his show, and he intended to run it his own way and without help from any of us. If he had Danny guarding Betsy during his absence, for instance, he'd tell us so when he was good and ready. All right, fine; I settled back to listen.

But he wasn't immediately done with me. A kind of chiding smile was on his lips as he said, "I understand, Sam, you chose not to mention to anyone that note you found."

"That's right," I said, while everybody else stared at me.

"This is the note I'm referring to," Clement said,

opening the small notebook he carried and taking out the piece of paper I'd last seen taped to the window in Jack French's room. Unfolding it, holding it at arm's length, he read the note aloud: "Stupid amateurs. By the time a real cop gets here, I'll be finished with all of you." He handed the note to Fred, nearest him on his right, saying, "It isn't signed, but it is clearly in Jack French's handwriting and employs the same green pen he apparently habitually used. Sam found it taped to a window in Jack's room."

Fred studied the note, with Crosby reading it over his shoulder. "I see," Fred said. With an enigmatic look in my direction, he passed the note on to George.

"Well, ain't that something," Crosby said, deadpan.

Bly gave me a frown of curiosity, then turned the other way to read with George, who said, "You mean, he's still in the house here, alive."

"Not exactly," Clement said.

Bly handed me the note, still giving me that same quizzical look. "I've seen it," I said, and handed it on to Harriet, who looked at me rather than at the note. She said, "Why didn't you tell us about it?"

"Because it's a fake," I said.

Clement laughed, a sudden barking sound. He looked briefly as though he might applaud. "You're absolutely right, Sam!" he said. "Full marks. I compared the note with the jottings Jack had made on that script up in his room, and the fact is, much of this note was *traced*. I found the words and parts of words that were used. I take it," he said to me, "you had some other reason for thinking it a fake."

"Only the fact that Jack French is dead," I told him.

"I'm glad you're so certain of that," he said. "And in fact, you're correct."

Harriet handed the note back to Clement, saying, "So this is meaningless."

"Well, no," Clement corrected her. "Nothing our murderer does is exactly meaningless. But the meaning, here as so often in this particular case, is something other than it at first appears. The meaning of this note is that the murderer wishes us—and eventually wishes the police as well—to *believe* that Jack French is alive, or at least that he was alive when this note was written. That he was alive, in fact, this morning, in order to commit the crime of murdering Mort Weinstein. In addition, it is my belief that this was only the first note we were to receive, purporting to be from Jack French. If everything had gone as the murderer had planned, we would have found a second note from Jack tomorrow morning. A suicide note, probably beside an open window. We would then be expected to believe that Jack French, unbalanced to begin with, driven over the edge by his journey here and the storm that overtook us, embarked on this rampage of murder, beginning with the woman to whom he had poured out his soul three years ago in Jamaica, continuing with Betsy—unsuccessfully, thank God—and then with Mort, intending to kill everyone on this island, and only at the end realizing the impossibility of what he was trying to do and the hopelessness of his position. In this scheme, we would have had a number of murders and attempted murders committed by an unbalanced man who eventually threw himself into the sea, leaving behind a convenient note, wrapping up the case in a tidy package for the police."

"It wouldn't have flown," I said.

"No, of course not," Clement said. "For a number of reasons."

"I can think of a couple myself," Fred said with another expressionless glance in my direction.

Harriet said with a hint of impatience, "Clement, you say the murderer was attempting an elaborate scheme to blame Jack French for his murders. Therefore, you say Jack French is not the murderer. Who do you say *is* the murderer?"

"Forgive me, Harriet," Clement said. "I truly don't wish to drag this out for dramatic effect, but if I were just to say a name now, this name or that name, everyone would insist on proof, reasons, justification, and we'd wind up doing the whole thing back to front. With your indulgence—with all of your indulgence—I would like to explain the situation in my own way."

"I don't suppose we have much choice," Harriet said, ostentatiously adjusting herself in her chair to be more comfortable over the long haul.

Clement apparently decided his dignity would be best served by ignoring the implications in that movement. Speaking generally, clasping the notebook to his breast again, he said, "The actual story begins, appropriately enough, with this house itself, the creation of the drug chieftain called Sonny Trager. He built this house, he designed it, he not only lived in it, but he also used it as a principal location in his business. Here in this house, cocaine was refined and prepared for smuggling into the United States."

I had no idea where Clement was ultimately headed, but I could see the next stop he was headed for along his route. Wanting to move things along more quickly, and also wanting to let Clement know he couldn't count too much on our indulgence, I said, "Clement, excuse me."

He looked in my direction with surprise and mild disapproval. "Yes?"

"If you're building up to tell us," I said, "that Danny Douglas is a dope dealer, we already knew that."

Bly stared at me once more. "*I* didn't know it," she said.

"Neither did I," Crosby said. "Are you sure?"

"Yes," I said. "Sonny Trager wanted somebody to take over this house while he was away. And, as Clement says, the house wasn't merely his home, it was also a major element in his business. He made a tricky and complicated deal with the federal investigators, where he gave them a lot of useful but probably smalltime information, and in return they let him pick the person who'd take control of this house. He chose Danny Douglas."

"Which Mort didn't like," Fred said. "He told me so, but he didn't tell me why."

I said, "Danny told me he and Mort were partners who didn't know much about each other's area of the partnership. Danny said he was Mr. Outside and Mort was Mr. Inside. Danny also told me there were Danmor Forever stars who had drug dealings with Sonny Trager, which was why Danny felt he had to go along with Trager's offer of the house. But Danny also told Bly and me that he'd known only one dope dealer in his life who wasn't himself a user, and when we asked who that was, he got coy and wouldn't answer."

Bly said, "He meant himself! Sure, he did. I *knew* there was something else going on there. Sam, why didn't you tell me all that?"

"I didn't realize it at the time," I told her, then said to the group, "Danny does what's necessary to keep his stars happy. He needs them, the company depends on them. He wants them happy, and he wants them safe. He doesn't want them getting arrested, jailed, any of that."

"Stay away from that moral turpitude clause," Fred suggested.

"That's right. So the best way to do that is to handle their drug business himself. Danny has total contempt for drugs and for people who get caught up with them, but they're such a part of the movie and TV business that he finally had to decide how best to handle the situation, and that's the way he chose."

Clement said a bit frostily, "Thank you, Sam. Yes, Danny has been a drug supplier, has actually carried cocaine and other substances to people's homes, has collected the money and paid Sonny Trager. And therefore, when Sonny Trager demanded that Danny become the caretaker of this house during Sonny's absence, Danny had no choice but to go along."

Fred said, "I noticed a lot of the equipment was still there in the refinery, ready to run again. Just add a couple missing pieces."

"Of course," Clement said.

I said to George, "That's what you didn't want to tell me about before, isn't it? That you quit working for Danny in Los Angeles because there were too many drugs around, it was too dangerous."

"A couple of times," George said, "Danny had me deliver little packages to people. I didn't like that one bit, I told him I don't want to do that. He said if he could—'' He broke off, and looked apologetically at Harriet. "Excuse, Miss," he said.

"Of course," Harriet said.

George went on. "Danny said if he could stand the smell of the shit, then I could too."

I told the group, "George quit Danny then, and didn't want to come back with him now—"

"I surely wish I hadn't," George said.

"But George needs the money," I finished, "because his wife has that baby on the way."

"Maybe already here," George said.

"And it was agreed this would only be a temporary job."

"That's right," George said.

"Then I think," Clement told us, lifting a finger to get our attention, "we can agree that Danny's status as drug dealer has been established. And also that his partner was unaware of much that was going on but disapproved of the part he knew."

Everybody acknowledged that we could agree on that much of his story. Once again in control, Clement went on to say, "But there was another area of trouble in the partnership as well, about which perhaps not all of us are aware."

He meant, of course, the embezzling of money from the stars they had under contract in TV series. He meant Mort's innocence and Danny's guilt and Mort's upcoming decision about whether or not to turn against his partner, a decision that had been overtaken by Mort's death. I could have interrupted again, of course, telling the same story much more briefly than Clement ever would, but I didn't. In the first place, it would have been rather snotty, when he was so relishing this turn as

the great detective, to keep running in with the astonishing news ahead of him every time. But more than that, I
didn't interrupt him because I saw at last where he was
heading, and I didn't like it, and I wanted time to think
about it.

He meant Danny. He was going to tell us all about
Danny's problems, and he was going to say that Danny
had killed Mort to save his own neck, and had done all
the rest of it to make it look as though a crazy man
named Jack French were the guilty party. And he was
wrong.

He was wrong because of my last conversation with
Danny, when I'd told him for sure that Jack French was
dead. Danny's reaction had not been that of a man who
desperately needed the fiction of Jack French still being
alive, in order to complete some scheme of his own.
Danny had talked like a man who knew all his dirty
linen was about to be aired and there was nothing to be
done about it. "Chickens coming home to roost," was
the way I'd described it to Bly.

Clement had been led astray by the fact that Danny
really *did* have a lot to hide, and really did have a
difficult relationship right now with his partner. Was the
relationship difficult enough to count as a motive for
murder? I thought it more likely that Danny was just
going along, one day at a time, hoping for the best.
He had not killed anybody, of that I was absolutely
certain.

So what would happen when Clement reached his
peroration, when he grandly threw open the curtain to
reveal his wrong answer? I'd have to disagree with him,
of course. Other people would too. Fred, for one, who
knew how the murderer had originally planned for Jack

French to be so melodramatically found, which wouldn't at all fit into the case Clement was making.

Why was he going out so far on the limb like this? Just for publicity for his new Sherlock Holmes TV series? Was he that worried about whether or not the show would make it?

Well, yes, he was.

Which would be the gentler way to let him down? Should I interrupt him now, or let him go through to the end? Either way, it would be horrible for him. As with so many totally self-involved people, his ego was both huge and incredibly fragile. Look at how carefully he'd dressed for this role, in gray slacks and sports jacket, that black cashmere scarf bunched under his chin like an ascot, setting off his aquiline features as he lectured us on the gentle art of murder.

I sat looking at him, not really listening to the words I'd already guessed were coming, my mind a jumble of thoughts as I delayed and delayed the inevitable moment when I would have to burst Clement's bubble; assuming no one else did it first.

But then, out of the confused clutter in my mind, one item popped to the surface, and I was so surprised by it that I immediately leaned forward and interrupted Clement without even thinking about it, saying, "Clement, may I look at that note again?"

He had his notebook open now, and was using some sort of outline in it to keep his story in sequence. Breaking off in mid-sentence, he frowned at me and said, "I beg your pardon?"

"The note from Jack's room. Could I see it?"

"Certainly." He found it in the notebook, removed it, handed it to me.

"Thank you."

He would have preferred to go right back to his recital, but of course everyone's attention was on me as I opened the note and once again read it through. Yes, that's what it said. I sighed, because the whole thing was so unnecessary.

Coldly, Clement said, "Well, Sam? Are you satisfied?"

"Yes," I said. "You can stop now. Danny Douglas didn't kill anybody."

He looked at me with some surprise. "I haven't said he did."

"No, but you're building up to it, and he didn't. Jack French isn't the crazed killer among us, and Danny isn't either."

Beside me, Bly reared back and looked at me as though not entirely sure she recognized me. She said, "You mean, you know who the killer is?"

"Yes," I said, but kept looking at Clement.

Did he see it coming? He met my eye without flinching, and gave me the straight line: "Who, Sam?"

I took it. "You, Clement," I said.

33

"**D**on't be ridiculous," he said, of course.

"The worst of it is," I said, "if I'd only thought a little faster, Danny would still be alive."

Everybody reacted to that, but it was George who spoke first, staring over at me, saying, "Danny? What's become of Danny?"

"Clement?" I said, looking at him. "Do you want to tell your version first?"

"I take it," he said with icy dignity, "you believe I have a version, and that you know it. I am prepared to defer to you."

"Tell," Bly said to me. "Now."

"To begin with what would have been Clement's story," I said, "he planned to tell you all that he'd worked it out that Danny was the killer, but as the last preliminary step before coming to us he confronted Danny with his conclusions, first establishing some sort of safeguard like a locked door. Danny's reactions, or his evasions, or confession, or whatever Clement decided on in his story, would be the final confirmation. Then Danny would have run off. Clement would have waited a bit, then carefully locked Betsy in and followed Danny and eventually found something similar to the note and the open window that he earlier described as being Danny's scheme for disposing of Jack French." Shaking my head at Clement, I said, "Sloppy plotting, Clement, using the same idea twice."

"I have no idea where Danny is," Clement answered stiffly. "But wherever he may be, alive or dead, he is most certainly the murderer we have all been seeking. I would have thought, Sam, that you would be, in a matter of this importance, above such displays of jealousy as to—"

"Oh, Clement, Clement," I said, feeling terribly sorry for him, "we weren't *all* seeking the murderer. Only you, Clement, were in that race."

"A slight contradiction there, I should think," he said. "First you accuse me of being the murderer, then you say I'm the only one trying to find the murderer."

Bly said, "Sam, what's *your* version? You say Danny's dead?"

"Yes," I said. "Clement killed him when Danny brought up his cocaine."

Which caused another stir, everybody but Harriet talking at once, Harriet simply gazing at me level-eyed to see whether or not I knew what I was talking about. When everybody else quieted down, I said, "Yesterday morning, I went into the kitchen and Danny was there, reading a cookbook. When he said hello to me, he almost shouted it, and I thought the acoustics in the kitchen must be strange, but after that there wasn't any shouting at all, and a while later Clement came out of the lavatory there, making some unnecessary explanation about stomach troubles that haven't seemed to bother him before or since.''

"This is the most asinine performance," Clement announced to the world, ''that I have ever been unfortunate enough to witness.''

"Clement, as we all know," I went on, "identifies himself rather completely with the character he usually plays. More, say, than Fred does, or Harriet, or I.''

Fred nodded, saying, "A lot more than me.''

Angrily, Clement glared at me, saying, "You would appear to *me* to be identifying rather pathetically at the moment with that television detective of yours.''

"Sherlock Holmes," I pointed out, "took cocaine, as we would now say, recreationally.''

Crosby said doubtfully, "Sam, excuse me a minute. Sure Clement does coke, you just have to look at his nose to see that, but—''

"I *beg* your pardon!" Clement reared back, staring in outrage at Crosby down the narrow length of the nose in question.

Crosby was unabashed. Giving Clement a look, she told him, "It wasn't always that skinny. You've been breaking down that wall in there, you know, not doing yourself any good at all.'' Turning back to me, while Clement stood speechless, she said, "Okay, Danny deals in it and Clement takes it. But Clement's *wife* is lying up there almost dead. You can tell me there was trouble between them if you want, and he's the one wanted to kill her—''

"No, I don't say that at all," I corrected her.

"Just a minute," she said. "Somebody did try to kill Betsy Hasbrouck. If it was Clement, like you say, then he's had almost twenty-four hours to finish the job, all alone in the room with the lady, and he didn't do it.''

"Exactly so," Clement said in gratitude, apparently forgiving Crosby for her earlier remarks about his nose.

I said, "Crosby, the way to look at that situation is like this: Betsy's the only victim who didn't die."

"And damn lucky too," Crosby said.

"No, wait, now," I said. "This murderer doesn't miss, except just that one time."

Crosby frowned at me. "Meaning what?"

"Meaning Clement wasn't trying to kill Betsy at all. He was trying to keep her alive without letting her talk to us, because—"

Clement overrode what I was trying to say, shouting, "Why do we have to listen to any more of this raving? The man is mad with jealousy, he's—"

Fred said, "Clement." He said it quietly, without inflection, but Clement stopped in mid-career and looked at him, and Fred said, still quietly, "Clement, I want to hear what Sam has to say."

"If you wish," Clement said coldly, and folded his arms and glowered in my direction.

I said, "The hardest place to keep a secret is inside a long-established couple. Two people who are linked together, living together, who know each other that well, find it very hard to keep secrets from each other."

"As adulterers," Fred said, "find out every day."

"Exactly." I said, "Betsy saw what Clement was up to, and she knew she couldn't let it go on. I don't know if she and Clement had a talk on the subject or what the mechanics of it were, but Clement realized he couldn't continue to go through with the plan, setting it up for Danny to take the rap and be conveniently dead—with the parallel in his plot that he'd claim Danny was trying to set it up for *Jack* to take the rap and be conveniently dead—Clement knew he couldn't go forward with that because Betsy would tell, Betsy would do whatever was necessary to stop him."

"That's all very—" Clement started, and Fred said, "Be quiet, Clement," and Clement stopped.

Bly said with shock in her voice, "Sam, are you saying Clement poisoned her, but not to kill her? To keep her *alive*?"

"If possible."

Shaking her head, she said, "I just can't believe it. That anybody would take a risk like that, with somebody they cared about . . ."

I turned to George, saying, "Was Clement one of the people Danny had you deliver packages to, maybe sometimes when you went over there to cook?"

"Sometimes," he admitted reluctantly, not looking in Clement's direction.

"So you knew Clement had a cocaine habit."

George looked uncomfortable, and remained silent.

Speaking generally, I said, "You have to count the cocaine in as a factor. Clement was desperate, and he was terrified. He'd gone too far to stop, but if he didn't stop, Betsy was prepared to tell everybody what was going on. He'd be ruined, he'd go to jail—or more probably the asylum—for the rest of his life. But if he *did* stop, with the scheme incomplete, the whole thing would unravel and he'd still be in just as much trouble, he'd still be caught. Think of the choice he had to make."

"This is beneath contempt," Clement said, but no one paid any attention.

I said, "I'm assuming Betsy figured out what was

going on, or part of it. Some error of Clement's did it, some moment when she knew he was in the wrong place, or something like that. She told him it had to stop, immediately, or she'd tell the rest of us the truth. Either she didn't realize he'd gone too far to turn back, or she didn't care. He was acting crazy, that's all she knew, but if he'd promise to stop it right there, she'd protect him until they got off the island. After that, she'd look for help, maybe from his doctor, maybe from somewhere else she had in mind.''

"Trying to salvage something," Fred suggested.

"Probably so. And she probably saw the choice she was giving him as 'Stop now or I'll tell the others what you're doing.' But Clement saw it was a much tougher choice than that. He had to either shut her up or get caught, no other way around it. At first, he would have seen the choice as between killing her or getting caught, and that would have been *really* difficult. But then he saw this possible other way. If he could just keep her quiet till he'd finished working out his scheme, there was still hope."

"But *how*?" Bly demanded. "What did he use? What did he give her?"

"I'm hoping Clement will tell us," I said, "now that it doesn't matter anymore. Because Betsy's surely in danger from whatever he's been doing to her."

But Clement wouldn't admit defeat. "Your suggestions," he told me, "are both ludicrous and offensive."

"Wait a minute," Crosby said, "wait a minute," and when I looked at her, she was frowning hard, thinking back. "You know," she said slowly, "you know, that always did look like some kind of OD, but I didn't see how it was possible."

I said, "Cocaine, you mean? Is that what he gave her?"

"No, no," she said, shaking her head, briskly getting rid of that idea. "Give a coke OD to somebody who doesn't use the stuff, they don't pass out, they start flying around the ceiling. This is more like, like, ummm, maybe a phenobarbital."

"And just where would I," Clement asked icily, "get such a thing?"

But suddenly Crosby smiled, and gave Clement a triumphant look, and said, "From Jack!"

Clement looked as startled as the rest of us. I said, "Crosby? From Jack French?"

"You saw that drugstore he had in the bathroom," she reminded us. "Pills and medicines, and some prescription stuff too. Wait a minute, I looked at them when we were up there, I can probably even tell you . . ." She frowned at Clement, trying to remember. "Was there Belladenal up there?"

"I really wouldn't know," Clement told her, but it seemed to me I saw something wary in his eyes as he watched her.

Crosby shook her head. "No, that wasn't it, but there was a GI prescription there, not tabs, a liquid—Donnatal!"

Clement jumped when she shouted that, then pretended he hadn't. I said, "Crosby? What's Donnatal?"

"Phenobarbital," she said, "other things, manufactured by Robins. It's for ulcer, bowel problems. You can cause coma with an overdose of that. And that's why her body temperature's so low. And it's not a tab, it's liquid, an elixir, easy to feed it to her. Easy to feed her more of it every time she starts to come around."

Looking wide-eyed at Clement, she said, "You're messing with that lady's insides."

Clement looked away from her, as though dismissively, but the gesture didn't quite come off. I said, "He never meant it to be for very long, just until he finished what he'd started. Keep Betsy unconscious, go into endgame— he's the one who called it endgame—present the Danny-as-murderer story to the police and have it accepted because the police would already have Danny-as-drug-dealer and Danny-as-embezzler, so why look any farther? And when Betsy came to at last in a hospital in New Orleans or Los Angeles, it would all be over, and at that point he'd be able to persuade her to keep his secret. There wouldn't be any reason to tell on him anymore, since he'd be finished, and he'd never do anything like that again. He was sure he could convince her, because it was the truth. So there he'd be, safe and sound, a media hero. The man who plays Sherlock Holmes *really* plays Sherlock Holmes, and comes up a winner."

Fred said doubtfully, "Sam, I've been wondering about motive. Is *that* what you have in mind? You say he was doing it for *publicity?*"

"Of course," I said.

Clement had begun to blink and twitch, folding and unfolding his arms as though he couldn't decide whether he was hot or cold. But he still kept his supercilious manner intact as he said, "How anyone could possibly believe for even a second that such a preposterous accusation would ever be given serious acceptance by anyone, just anyone at all, never mind the police, I really don't know. To think—"

Harriet, nodding thoughtfully, as though Clement

weren't speaking at all, said, "He planned it that first day, didn't he?"

"I suppose so," I said, while Clement stopped talking to stare at her.

Harriet nodded again, agreeing with herself. "Yes, that's how it would have been," she said. "He came here already unbalanced, afraid of being a has been, knowing this television series was his absolute last chance and that it was a desperate gamble on everybody's part, the likelihood was that it would fail, as other programs on that network in that time slot had failed. But the network would merely replace Sherlock Holmes with another series, while Clement would be finally and irrevocably destroyed. He had to be Sherlock Holmes, or he was no one."

I said, "Yes, I think that's the way it was with him."

"The drugs would have helped to push him along," she said. "And the difficult flight, coming in. But the death of the pilot was what tipped the balance. You could see it happening, couldn't you? That first day."

"We could," I agreed. "But we had no way to know what it was."

"Of course not," she said. "Merely the idea being raised by Crosby, in this room, that the pilot might have been murdered. That's what put the idea in his mind, put that little worm in there to eat its way through his reason."

"By golly," Fred said, "I remember how he loved that idea."

"Yes," Harriet said, nodding at him, "it excited him, fevered him. The rest of us left the observation room eventually that time, but Clement remained behind, thinking, brooding. 'If it were murder,' he told himself over and over, 'and if I could solve it, *that* would give the show a boost!' That's the way he would have thought of it at first.''

Bly said, "But it wasn't murder. Was it?"

"No, of course not," Harriet answered. "The pilot died an accidental death. But there was Clement," she went on, her rich actress's voice deepening, rolling out as though across footlights, "there he was," she told us, gesturing to paint the scene, "in the observation room, all alone, the storm raging silently around him, the ocean before him where the plane had gone in, and his mind was full to bursting with *if only if only if only*." She leaned forward, like all three witches in Macbeth, fixing us one at a time with her strong gaze. "But it wasn't murder," she told us, "and even if it had been murder, Clement had no way to solve it. So he came away from there at last to dinner, still brooding, still worried about his future, but seeing at last the *manner* in which he might be saved, if not yet the specifics." She turned her eyes on me. "Isn't that the way you see it, Sam?"

"Yes," I said.

"Yes." She glanced almost indifferently at the silent staring mesmerized Clement, then continued, speaking to the rest of us. "Clement saw that his salvation lay in *solving a murder*. If the actor playing Sherlock Holmes could actually solve a murder, what a coup that would be! The media would love it. The show would be well and truly launched. Clement's life—his life as Sherlock Holmes—would be saved."

"That's exactly right," I said. "That's what started him on the way."

"That evening," Harriet continued, and paused, and

touched her fingertips to her brow. Everyone remained silent while a wave of pain crossed her features, half hidden by her hand. Then she took a deep breath, lowered her hand, raised her face, and went on. "That evening, at dinner, there was a certain amount of drama. Later on, Clement would combine those two things, the death of the pilot and Daphne's"—we waited a long while for Harriet to choose a word, and at last she did—"tantrum. He would combine them, and put them at the service of his need to solve a murder."

I said, "I think I know what happened in that part. It was Betsy who went upstairs with Daphne and spent the evening with her. Generally, husbands and wives discuss interesting events together, so when Betsy finally left Daphne that night, she would naturally tell Clement all about it while they were settling down for bed."

There was a low sofa behind Clement, who had been standing all this while. Now, with a sweeping gesture that was meant to be an ironic the-stage-is-yours, but which was marred by a distinct trembling of the hand, he backed to this sofa and settled down on it with a great deal of dignity, stony-faced. His manner was meant to suggest that he was prepared to wait until these silly immature people had done with their pointless and puerile attacks. It would have been more convincing if he hadn't been trembling quite so hard.

I said, "Betsy would have told Clement the state she'd left Daphne in, that it seemed to her there was a real worry that Daphne might take her own life—"

"She never would," Harriet said firmly.

"Nevertheless," I said, "Daphne had in fact that night threatened suicide, in Betsy's presence. So that made it another death portending, like the pilot's, but just as useless from Clement's point of view."

"Useless," Harriet murmured. "I like that word. Yes, that's what Clement was thinking."

"The difference being," I said, "that this death hadn't yet happened. Clement could influence it. The apparent accident had already occurred and actually was an accident, and there was nothing to be done about it. But the suicide didn't exist yet. Clement would *make* it happen, he could make something that would look like the expected suicide, but with small anomalies within it, little clues that only he would notice, because he would have put them there. So that's what he did. The feather. The torn pillowcase."

With something like awe in her voice, Bly said, "That has to be one of the strangest motives in the history of the world. He committed a murder in order to solve it."

"And I suppose," Harriet said, "he planned at first to blame it on Jack French."

"Well, no," Fred said. "He had other ideas for Jack, but they didn't pan out."

I saw Clement give Fred a hard and speculative look, but I didn't follow through on that because another thought had occurred to me. "I'm remembering," I said, "the last thing Danny said to me. We'd been talking about his legal problems, and his problems with his partner, and his hope that Jack French was still alive somehow and was the murderer. When I told him there was no hope from that quarter, Jack French was definitely dead, he said that meant he probably knew who the killer was, but the knowledge wouldn't help him. Then he went away, because Clement had called him.

He brought Clement his cocaine, and told him he now knew Clement was the killer, and that's why Clement altered his plans yet again. He killed Danny right away, and came down here to make his great revelations now rather than at dinner, the way he'd originally intended.''

"Very adaptable, our Clement," Fred said.

"Very," I agreed.

Harriet said, "You mean, he changed his plans along the way?"

"Several times," I told her. "But I think he had it in mind to discover that Danny was the killer from the very beginning. He had to choose somebody, and Danny was the one with the most legal problems already, the one with the strongest motive for killing *somebody*. That he had no motive for killing Daphne could be worked out eventually."

"How?" Harriet demanded. "If Danny were to murder somebody, it would be Mort."

"But when the idea formed in Clement's mind," I said, "Daphne was the clearest target of opportunity. I don't suppose he feels like telling us right now what he hoped to accomplish, how he expected to link it all together, but one way would be that Mort had discussed the problems with Jack French, who had discussed them with Daphne—links among those three had already been established—so they were the three people with knowledge dangerous to Danny. The idea would have been that Danny hoped to pass off Daphne's death as suicide, but that when that didn't work, because of Clement's brilliant deductions, Danny then decided to kill Jack French in such a way as to make it seem that Jack was the killer himself, hiding somewhere in the house."

Fred said, "That couldn't have been the original plan."

"No," I agreed. "But Clement's had so many different plans and schemes, there's no way to sort them out. He's been scrambling ever since he started this thing."

Bly said, "Sam, what about that note? Why was it the note that made you think Clement was the killer? It was just a threat, that's all, supposed to be from Jack."

"But again," I said, "with a flaw in it for Clement, the brilliant detective, to discover. That the words had been traced from another example of Jack's writing. What Clement didn't realize was that there was one *more* flaw in the note, a flaw that proves which person in the house actually wrote it."

Bly said, "I give up. What was it?"

"In the note," I explained, "we are as a group insulted, called stupid amateurs who will all be dead by the time the real police get here. Now, only Clement and Betsy were missing from this room when Fred announced to everybody that I used to be a policeman a long time ago. Anybody else who had written that note, including Danny, would have phrased it differently."

Clement stared at me as though I'd just committed a horribly ungentlemanly breach of proper conduct. "You were *what*?" he demanded.

Fred laughed, an unusually harsh sound from that round and amiable face. "We aren't playing fair, Clement," he said. "We *aren't* all amateurs. Sam used to be a local cop on Long Island."

Clement looked at me hard, trying to fit this new Sam Holt into his scenario. "That makes no difference," he decided at last. "Years ago, you said. That's probably what Danny meant, when he wrote that. You *were* in the police, but so long ago you're not a real policeman anymore. That's why he talked about *real* police."

Crosby, sounding extremely impatient, said, "Clement, why don't you get *off* this? You're caught, man, it's all over, give it up."

But Clement wasn't about to do that. Seated on the sofa, he drew himself up and in, making his body and brain rigid against our attacks. Switching his glare to Crosby, he said with an effort at icy self-assurance, "What a wonderful framework of nonsense you have all put together, while I've been sequestered with Betsy. But it *is* nonsense, I assure you. Danny Douglas was the murderer in our midst, and no other. You have theories, jealous nonsensical theories, and that's all. Where is the slightest bit of physical proof? There is none. None!"

"Actually," I said, "there is."

He gave me a wary look, afraid of me now. "There can't be," he said.

To Fred, I said, "You remember, we both said it was too bad Mort wasn't just a little faster in defending himself, fast enough to leave some sort of mark on his attacker. Clement has been wearing that black scarf tucked up under his chin all day. When he takes it off, in a minute, we'll all see the bruises on his throat where Mort grabbed him, just before Clement finally managed to get in the knife-thrust that finished the job."

"Nonsense, nonsense, all nonsense," Clement cried, but his voice croaked, it squeaked as though it were rusty. And his trembling right hand went up to the scarf, holding it close to his throat.

Bly said slowly, "I guess it must be true. But it's so hard to see it, to visualize Clement Hasbrouck with a knife in his hand, stabbing somebody to death."

Fred told her, "You think that's something? You

should have seen what he did to Jack French. I can visualize this cokehead doing *anything*.''

With wonder in his face, Clement turned toward Fred, staring at him. He even stopped trembling. "*You* moved Jack?'' he demanded. "*You* did? But why? It was so beautiful!''

34

Even after that, he tried to go on with the denials, to the point of actually denying his sudden exclamation to Fred about Jack's body: "I never said any such thing! Never! You're twisting my words!"

We very nearly had to twist his arm to get him to take off the black scarf. "You'll believe what you want to believe," he insisted, his right hand pressed splay-fingered to the scarf, just below his concealed Adam's apple. "I had a fall in the tub, there may be—"

"Oh, Clement, *stop* it!" Crosby cried, exasperated beyond endurance.

Others of us had things to say as well, overriding Clement's increasingly absurd and desperate maneuvers, but it was George who brought that particular impasse to an end. Leaning forward, his left hand stretched out palm upward toward Clement, he said, "May I take your scarf, Mr. Hasbrouck?"

Was that the moment when Clement gave up? His manner remained cold and haughty, but it seemed to me something shriveled behind his eyes as he looked at George, sitting there so calmly and respectfully, the good servant, with his hand patiently out, waiting. Looking at George, but speaking to us all, Clement at last said, "You can say what you want to say. You can believe what you want to believe." He removed the scarf, ruffling his hair on the left side as he lifted the cloth over his head, so that for the first time he looked like somebody with madness inside. Then he reached out, the ends of the black scarf dangling away between his fingers to trail on the floor, the dull gray bruises on his throat a sullen contrast with the pallor of his skin. Handing the scarf to George, he said, "I shall not speak on this subject again."

Nor did he. When it became clear that his tactic now was to remain mute, we turned instead to the question of what to do with him between now and whenever tomorrow a plane would arrive. We talked about him as though he weren't present, and in a way he wasn't, having closed himself in behind that stony facade.

It was clear we couldn't just let him wander around on his own for the next fifteen or eighteen hours, but it was less clear what we should do with him instead. Merely locking him into one of the unused bedrooms presented the problem that he might decide to commit suicide some time during the night, once he'd worked out for himself the hard truth that there would be absolutely no wriggling out of it this time. But on the other hand, none of us was particularly interested in spending our time on a suicide watch.

It seems foolish to say we'd lost sympathy with Clement—he was, after all, a multiple murderer—but I do think that's precisely the way we felt. None of us were by this stage horrified or repelled by him, we weren't angry or vengeful, we were just simply out of patience with this shallow, frivolous man. His self-absorption had become so complete that no one else in the world, with the partial exception of his wife, had any reality or meaning in his brain at all anymore. If he was mad, it was a self-induced madness, brought on by ego and drugs, and not worthy of our pity.

That may have been why it all ended as it did, I don't know. I don't believe we were consciously aware that it wasn't over yet, that there was one more step to go before the game was done. We were just fed up with Clement, that's all, annoyed by his demand that we should take his stupidity seriously, while he didn't even take the fact of our existences seriously. Maybe at some unconscious level we had all begun to see him as we now understood he had all along seen us. That might explain it.

On the surface, though, we remained for the most part rational and caring beings. In the discussion of where we should keep Clement until the police arrived, Harriet's suggestion that we store him in Sonny Trager's dungeon at the bottom of the building was met with immediate and loud rejection. I'm probably not the only one who thought at first she wasn't serious, and it was only when she pressed her arguments in favor of the dungeon that I saw in her flinty-eyed face that she was in dead earnest. "We need a secure room," she said, "without a window, so he can't throw himself out. And with solid locks. What better than the dungeon?"

"Harriet," I said, "that's an inhuman place down there. We aren't going to put Clement or anybody else in a room like that."

"I don't see why not," she said.

George said, "There's a pantry at the back of the kitchen, it used to be the wine cellar, it's empty now. The door locks, and there's no window."

I remembered the room he was talking about, from our second search for Jack French. Two of the walls were stone, the others ordinary Sheetrock. A pair of pinlights set into the ceiling provided the only illumination. There were built-in wooden shelves along one side, but no furniture, and the only entrance was through a plain flush door from the rear of the kitchen, past the small lavatory. Because it had been Sonny Trager's wine cellar, it had a pretty good Yale-type lock on it. "That's good," I said. "We can put a chair and a mattress in there for Clement for tonight."

"Why?" said Harriet.

No one answered her. I suppose we all thought it a rhetorical question.

I'd expected it would be difficult to actually move Clement into that pantry, but he gave no trouble at all. When we told him it was time to go, he rose, stiffly but under complete control, and gave each of us a look of withering contempt before turning on his heel and striding off to the kitchen, George and I following. His manner showed the line he would take from now on; that he had fallen among knaves and fools and would have nothing more to do with them, but would wait until he could tell his story to solid rational professionals. There was no way his story would fly with rational professionals, of course, but it would be better for all of us, Clement included, if he could go on conning himself at least through tonight into the belief that he still had some hope.

When we got to the kitchen, I said, "I'm sorry, Clement, but I'm going to have to ask you to empty your pockets. Just put everything on the counter here."

Again he obeyed, and again with that look of venomous scorn. Wallet, change, pocket knife, notebook, two pens, magnifying glass, handkerchief, a box of small wooden matches, a syringe in a flat plastic case, a compartmented silver box containing various pills, a pair of reading glasses, a small roll of string, and a comb, which he ran through his hair before putting with the rest on the butcher block counter, where they all made a sad little pile under the kitchen fluorescents.

I thought he might give trouble when I asked for his shoes and belt as well, but after a brief tense moment of deliberation, he decided dignity would be better served by giving in.

The pantry was small and narrow, but livable for one night. In his socks, holding his trousers with his left hand, Clement went on in without argument. "I'll bring you a chair and a mattress in a little while," I told him from the doorway.

He ignored me, but stood gazing intently at the room, as though it were vitally important that he memorize it in the shortest possible time. I locked him in, pocketed the key, and George and I went off to one of the empty bedrooms for a mattress and pillow and two blankets. That, plus a chair from the dining room, would be Clement's furnishings for the night.

He still stood in the same place, and continued to ignore us, as we brought the things in and laid the mattress out on the floor. I tried to find something to say to him before again locking him in, but there was nothing.

Back in the observation room, I found Bly and Fred standing at the windows, looking out at a fairly astonishing sight. The trailing edge of the storm was still with us, the surface of the sea wind-tossed and agitated, the sky tumbling with dirty clouds, but far away on the southwestern horizon there was now a band of yellow light, like a line of crayon drawn to separate sea from sky. "Correct me if I'm wrong," Bly said to me. "Isn't that what we used to call sunlight?"

"I have a vague memory," I agreed.

"I thought so." She hooked an arm in mine. "So we're going to have an actual sunset. I bet a good one, too, with all those clouds."

"Good. Where are the others?"

Fred said, "Crosby went up to look at Betsy. I had to pry the door open. But Crosby says, now she knows what it is, she knows what to do about it."

"Clement took such a terrible chance with her," Bly said.

I said, "Clement took terrible chances all over the place."

"And they didn't work."

"No."

"Harriet went up to her room to rest," Fred said. "To be alone for a while mostly, I think."

"That's natural."

"Sure." He said, "And we found the open window, and the note from Danny."

"If only I'd thought a little faster," I said. "Once I knew it was Clement, that meant he *had* to kill Danny to get himself out from under. I just didn't dope it out soon enough."

"Well, how could you?" Bly asked me. "Before Clement started *his* version."

"The note," I told her. "I should have seen what it meant the instant I found it, that the phrasing eliminated everybody but Clement."

"I have to tell you," Fred said, "I keep wondering, if you'd showed me that note or told me about it, instead of keeping it to yourself, would *I* have doped it out."

"I know," I said. "I don't feel good about that."

"Well, what I think is," Fred went on, "if this will make you feel any better, I'm pretty sure I *wouldn't* have seen it." Grinning at me, he dropped into his Charlie Chan. "Wise man who know limits of own wisdom not likely to fall off edge."

"Thanks, Fred," I said. "I appreciate that."

"Oh, it's sincere," Fred told me.

"Sunshine," Bly said, looking out the window.

35

I hadn't expected Harriet to come down and join us for the dinner George put together, but she did, silent and thoughtful, so we were nearly a full complement of six around the table, with George and Harriet and Fred and Crosby and Bly and me. It was a quiet meal, not even Fred making any attempts at light conversation, though Crosby did tell us about the condition of her "patient," Betsy. "She's still out, but she's comfortable," Crosby said in satisfaction. "Now that I know what it is, and now that nobody's giving her any *more* of that stuff, she'll be all right. Sometime tomorrow she ought to wake up and come out of it fine."

"Except," Bly said, "for what she'll wake up to."

"Poor lady," Crosby agreed.

"The survivors," Harriet said without expression, looking at her plate, "take longer to die." No one found anything to say to that.

After dinner, George went off to see if Clement wanted anything to eat, Harriet went back up to her room, and

Fred and Crosby and Bly and I went as usual out to the observation room, where the darkness had once more turned the place into a self-observation room. We did try to look out, all of us wanting to see the storm depart, but all we could see was our own intent and shadowed faces, so we gave it up and made ourselves drinks, and sat in a circle to talk.

With the slaughter at last over, and Harriet's grim grief no longer directly in front of us, we could allow ourselves to relax, even to laugh. Fred told anecdotes about going on the road, doing personal appearances as Charlie Chan; Bly found pop culture references to everything everybody said; and Crosby and I rang in with occasional stories and remarks of our own. It was almost like being in a sane and rational world again.

Sometime later, George came out to tell us that Clement had eaten heartily but silently, had used the lavatory next door to his temporary prison, and had been locked in for the night. He was, according to George, maintaining his stiff-backed manner of offended hauteur, and hadn't deigned to say a word. Nor had he offered any resistance, though given the relative sizes and physical states of George and Clement, that wasn't exactly a surprise.

"So that's it for tonight," George finished, and extended his hand toward me with the small key in his palm. "Do you want to keep this?"

The key had been in the lock on the outside of the pantry door when we'd first put Clement in there, and George had been carrying it ever since. "No," I said, "you hold on to it. You'll be the first one in the kitchen in the morning, you'll want to deal with him then."

He looked doubtful, and continued to show me the

key on his palm. Slowly, he said, "I'm not sure, you know, that I want the responsibility."

I said, "Come on, George, there's no problem. Clement's safe in there until help gets here in the morning. It's all over."

Well, of course, it wasn't.

36

When the knock on the bedroom door woke me from troubled sleep, I knew immediately what it meant. "Hell," I said, sitting up. "She killed him." Bright early-morning sunlight leaked past the edges of the shades drawn over the windows.

Bly rolled over to look at me. "What?"

Tattered shreds of dreams fell away from my mind. I felt as though I'd been dreaming about this last death all night. "Be right there," I called at the door, and got out of bed.

Bly sat up, wide awake. "What is it, Sam?"

"Clement's dead," I said, pulling on my robe, kicking into my slippers.

She stared at me, then at the door, then at me again. "He is? How do you *know*?"

"I just do," I said, and went out, closing the door behind me.

George was in the vestibule, worried-looking. "Mr. Li will be right with us," he said.

"It's Clement, isn't it?"

He shook his head, but not to disagree with me. "I knew I didn't want that key."

"It won't be a problem," I told him, as the other bedroom door opened and Fred came out, his round face unnaturally grim.

George, trying to be hopeful, said, "Maybe it's just his heart stopped."

"Oh, his heart stopped, all right," I said. "The question is, what stopped it."

Fred said, exactly as I had, "It's Clement, isn't it?"

I agreed it was Clement, and we all trooped away downstairs.

Although our concentration was on that pantry ahead of us, it was impossible not to be aware of the windows we went past along our way, and the deep change that had taken place in the environment outside this building. As though the storm had never been, as though no storm had ever happened in the history of the world, the whole blue sky seemed to shine down, giving off a glow like a healthy face. A different sea surrounded us now, a glimmering green touched with the very lightest of brushmarks in white, then shading away in the distance to a royal blue that seemed to draw its strength from the paler blue of the sky. Two small white cotton puffs of cloud far away to the east emphasized the clear and perfect emptiness of the bowl above us. White-yellow sunlight that flickered and danced on the wavelets made the ocean look as though it were laughing.

George had left the key in the lock of the pantry door, representing his desire not to be a part of all this. Inside, in fluorescent lighting that seemed harsh and uncaring after the glimpses of sun outdoors, Clement lay on his side on the mattress we'd brought, one blanket beneath him, the other above. His jacket and shirt and trousers were hung neatly on the chair. In the cold light, Clement's face looked gray, almost blue.

He wasn't entirely cold, the waxy skin of his throat still retaining a memory of the warmth of life. His eyes were closed, his mouth slightly agape. There was still flexibility in his shoulder when I reached under the blanket to move his arm. "An hour," I said. "Two hours at the most. Around sunrise, I suppose."

"Mmm," Fred said, leaning over the body, bracing himself with a hand against the wall.

I followed the line of his gaze, and saw the dark blood in Clement's ear, a tiny crater lake of it; the only sign. "Like that," I said.

"Like that," Fred agreed.

George stood watching us, bewildered, and afraid to open his mouth. Fred and I left the pantry and crossed the kitchen together to the wall-mounted key rack. Fred opened its door, and we stood looking at the keys in there, dangling from their tiny hooks with the writing in black marker pen above each, saying what it opened. The hook marked WINE CELLAR was empty. "Well, that's stupid," Fred said, sounding surprised.

"No, wait," I told him, and stepped back to look at the keys from a little way off. On some of the hooks were two or three keys, on others there were none. After a minute I saw it, a little brighter than the others. "Try that one," I said, moving forward again, pointing at it, where it peeked from behind the duller key whose hook it shared.

"Oh, sure," Fred said, seeing the one I meant. "It's been cleaned." He took the key over to the pantry door, removed the one George had left in the lock, tried the new one, and it worked. Bringing it back, he said to me, "Why move it?"

"Scared," I suggested. "Overly emotional afterward, starting to break down."

Holding the key, Fred looked upward. "Do you think there's a problem?"

"No," I said. "And if there is, it's over by now."

Fred put the key where it belonged. His fingers had dulled it slightly, but it still looked to me like the only key in the cabinet that had been scrubbed to remove fingerprints. Well, it wasn't likely to matter.

I closed the key rack door, and Fred went over to open drawers in the work counter. He lifted a skewer, then an icepick. "Something like this," he said.

"They'll all be clean. There's no telling which."

"Still," he said, "here they are." He put them back into their drawer and closed it. "I don't like that blood," he said.

I said, "George, would you go up and tell Bly and Crosby that everything's okay?"

He was glad to go, but at the same time curious. "You want me to come back here, then?"

"No need," I told him. "We'll leave Clement right where he is and lock up again."

"I don't know about breakfast," he said. "I don't know if I feel like working in here."

Fred said, "We'll make coffee. That's all anybody wants anyway."

George left, at last. Fred took the roll of paper towels, I chose a tiny demitasse spoon from a drawer, and we went back to the pantry. With the handle end of the spoon, I gently worked the coagulated blob of blood out of Clement's ear. Fred used corners of paper towel, moistening them with his tongue, to finish the job, then said, "Anything else?"

"No."

We stayed a moment, hunkered together over Clement's body, our heads very close. Looking at me, Fred said, "They'll do an autopsy, you know."

"Larger facts than this have disappeared," I said, "when it seemed a good idea."

"Sometimes," said Fred's Charlie Chan, "much knowledge *also* dangerous thing."

"I wouldn't know," I told him, and he grinned and nodded.

Back in the kitchen, I washed the spoon and Fred flushed the paper towels away in the lavatory toilet and we made coffee. We carried two trays out to the observation room, one with coffee and milk and sugar, the other with cups and spoons. Alone out there, surprisingly, was Harriet, seated in a chair with a good view of the fine day. She looked at us, her face blank, and said, "Good morning."

"Good morning."

"Everything all right?"

"Everything's fine," I told her.

"Coffee?" Fred asked her.

She seemed a bit surprised, then thoughtful, then blank again. "Coffee would be fine," she said. Facing the windows, she said, "A plane is coming."

It was. We stood and watched it circle toward us through the invisible air.